I0670951

The Whole Package II
Table of Contents

Prelude

This Sequel begins with returning home from an adventure of a lifetime. Getting to know you better was the plan now. The gifts from GOD were slowly being integrated between this new / old couple. I refer to it being old because this was a plan from the beginning.

Football is the center of Sam's plan. He now has his cake and he's eating it too! Sam touches many people's lives on his way to his destiny in this life. He's also enjoying the company of his version of a real woman that was made for him! Marriage isn't out of the question. Sam and Fro's families will increase surprisingly! Fro can no longer hide her light! She touches as many people as Sam. She also has a large extended family.

Business picks up in their personal lives. Fro helps with Sam's businesses when he has to be with the Football team. Their ability to speak without words makes a big difference in business transactions. Sam can take action in real-time on important decisions that Fro relays during meetings on his behalf. Their Twin Flame status affords this gift. They have functional, true love for each other. There's power in a love like that.

This book is written from an epic dream and is fiction
(**Fiction** defined; Literature that is a work of the imagination
and is not necessarily based on fact)
Its rating is GC (May Contain Graphic Content).

Names, characters, places and incidents are product of the
author's imagination or are used fictitiously. The author's
dream/fantasy may have been inspired in part by her own
personal desires.   Any resemblance to actual events or locals or
persons living or dead, is entirely coincidental and are intended
to give the novel a sense of reality.

For information contact; **wholepkg_fro@cox.net**

Copyright @ 2015   The Whole Package II by Frozine Slater-Morrow
ISBN 13: 978-0-9986303-1-1
ISBN: eBook pending
LCCN: 2017911286

Cover design: **covers_fro@cox.net**
Cover photograph: FSM/CCM
Photographs are sole property of FSM
This sequel novel is being presented by Divine Providence.

First Printing FEBRUARY 2015
Manufactured and Published July 2017 in Virginia Beach, Virginia
Printed in the United States of America by Lulu, Inc. of Raleigh,
North Carolina 27607

THE WHOLE PACKAGE II

By

Frozine Slater-Morrow

The gift of Healing is an awesome responsibility. The Holy Spirit is depended upon for guidance. Everyone isn't supposed to be healed. Some afflictions are allowed. GOD uses those whom he called however He wants. If there were no afflictions, there would be no need for healing! There would be less opportunity for talking with GOD. The GOD I know says He's *jealous*! He wouldn't devise a plan that lets His people spend limited time with Him.

Sam and Fro are tuned in to GOD! There is purpose for their lives. They are walking in GOD's Divine Providence. All while coaching football, having private companies, introducing miracle hair care and body homeopathic products that work, caring for children and students and having the best sex and human love affair available on earth. What if this is not just a dream but someone's real life? It's encouraging to my soul to know that no matter where I am in life, I can plead my case to the Creator and if I try to live right, He will hear my cry and send HELP!

There's a message in this dream for someone other than me. I'm a messenger in this with words that are not mine. Remembering the cliché, 'Don't kill the messenger! She's on a mission from The Creator!'

Thanks for reading this tale. If this message is for you, well, **YOU"VE BEEN SERVED**!

Love Frozine

Vacation Was Over

Sam would be leaving to go home to his house in Charlottesville. It was a two and a half hour drive from Virginia Beach.

He helped carry the crates inside and through the house to the back yard. We took all of my things out of the truck so they wouldn't be left in the heat.

Sam wanted to go upstairs to rest before his trip home after dinner. My youngest wasn't home yet. I was a little nervous because I had not had another man in my bedroom. I believe Sam is marking his ground. I had already replaced the bed. I did promise to date him. We took off our clothes and got into bed. Without my help, Sam made love to me. He was good at controlling my body's reaction to him.

We talked to my daughter during dinner and let her know Sam and I would be dating. She took it better than I expected. Sam told her I was coming to stay at the college with him after she graduates. She said, 'really.' He told her she needed to come to UVA too.

Enroll in school there so we could all still be together. She thought that was a good idea.

Sam told her he would be back next week for training camp with the team. He wanted to stay with us instead of a hotel.

He asked if she wanted to make money that week driving, carrying his stuff and running errands. He told her he would pay her five hundred dollars for the week and she could drive his car with COACH tags. She jumped at it. He was teaching her how to get up front and close parks as well as valet. This man was setting up his place in my daughter's life. Smart move!

He reminded me that he really needed me to go back to Cozumel with him in three weeks.

He also reminded me that my husband was no longer among the living and will not return in this life. I was his woman now, until death or we meet GOD!

When we got back from dinner, Sam left for his home. It was hard seeing him leave because we had been together for so many days straight.

Of course he spoke with me without words but it was not the same as touching him.

After a few days he called me on the phone. It was Saturday morning. He said he didn't have anything to do until Monday. He asked if he could stay with us until Sunday night. I agreed. He was there in two hours. He had to be speeding. We enjoyed each other's company.

We spoke about how he wanted me to help with the businesses so I would have to completely leave my current job. He wanted more hands on so he asked me to be at meetings when he couldn't. He was preparing for football season and it would take all of his time.

He wanted me to check on Jacob in Jamaica and make sure Michael was straight. Michael needed assistance with acquiring new contracts.

Carlo needed someone to speak with the workers and help build morale. I could do that. Sam said he needed me to meet with a few new contacts.

I would soon be putting in my own request to have services in both businesses but needed to get use to the businesses and people first. I would be staying at Sam's places in Jamaica and Cozumel.

At the upcoming Cozumel meeting, Sam wanted me to go so I could see how he handled things and duplicate it later. I agreed. Sam would be flying us to Cozumel himself in a few weeks. This will be interesting.

It was still summer and I would have to find a place for my daughter to go. I was not ready to take her with Sam and me yet. I was just learning him myself. I wasn't ready to fully trust him with my youngest. Time will tell.

Summer Football Camp/We're Dating Now

It was finally Sunday before camp starts. The team was lodging in Virginia Beach and practicing at the local Sports center for a week. Sam was staying with us. After he got the team and assistant coaches settled, he called me. My daughter answered. She said okay and hung up. She told me Sam was on his way. When he arrived we kissed passionately. My daughter came up and hugged him too. He was happy. He took his things to my room, then checked the refrigerator for drinks and noted our house was small but cozy. He felt like relaxing here. I was happy to hear this.

I wanted to make love but my daughter was two rooms away. It had been so free on the ship to make as much noise as we wanted to but now I didn't want to startle my child. Sam said he would kiss me so the sound would be absorbed by him. I responded, 'sure you're right.' I made dinner for us. First time I cooked for him and knew it was Sam I was sharing food with.

My daughter left with friends to go to the movies. This gave us a chance to talk.

I had not exactly had a chance to process all that happened while we were away. We sat down and had a long talk. I made a list and wanted to be clear I was not imagining this.

Nan had exposed me to natural elements as well as rum and coffee. The shampoo, conditioner, tortoise cream, lotion and conch oil alone were priceless. Women and men alike would pay dearly for their hair to grow, let alone allow kinky hair to become more manageable without chemicals. Sandy could make a fortune. We would have to have a large enough quantity to make any dent in the business it could generate. The tortoise cream and lotion would make millions if sold. The conch oil could keep a lot of men at home with their own woman if used properly.

The rum was already being sold in the US. They had it at the club in Miami. The rum cream could sell itself. I asked Sam would Nan and Poppy allow me to be a distributor? He said I would have to ask them.

He said they want what money can't buy. I already knew this answer. They had taken Sam's mothers place in his life. Grandchildren or a grandchild is what they really wanted! With me already being fifty years old and no uterus, we would have to have someone else carry our child, if we had one. Sam reminded me that Sandy would do it if we asked her and we were ready. The child or children would be our natural child or children. Would we do that and give it or them to Nan and Poppy to care for? Maybe just temporary. That would be a hard decision. One I was not making now. Sam agreed.

We went in the backyard to smoke. Sam said he would not be smoking from August-February (Football Season). It sounded like a good idea but I wasn't making the same commitment. I would be cutting back considerably but there may be times when a little puff, puff pass would save me or someone else. Besides I still had a few joints from the different islands. I asked Sam about Jacob's collection and how I fit there.

He said I should sport his clothing style until I had enough people asking about where to get the styles. He said, 'Again, this is Jacob's call. You have to work that out with Jacob.'

He told me he admired me for the way I took the knowledge of Jacob and his tail. Sam said he would not be comfortable with most outsiders and how they may judge Jacob or him for that matter. He squeezed my thigh and smiled. I told him I would be using Mimi for sure. He said she would like that.

I was already tired of talking and needed or wanted to be with Sam like we had been before. Being home made this whole situation real. I was with a man who loved me and I felt the same. I told Sam it was nice being with him but he had to understand I was not moving or leaving my home until my daughter graduated next year. He said he knew. I told him I'll help with the businesses but could not be gone for long periods of time, leaving my daughter at home. He reminded me that he needed and wanted me not to change.

I was happy to hear this. We rubbed each other in all the right spots and I took advantage and sat on his little friend right in the back yard. It was fun sneaking that way. I didn't move much. It was nice being connected.

It started to feel like his little friend was getting his own freak on without my or Sam's help. Felt weird but nice at the same time. Sam didn't say anything. He just held me close. This first night felt strange and a little uncomfortable but better during the middle of the week.

My daughter was having fun helping the team. I'm sure they were enjoying her also. What's not to like about a cheerleader? Sam communicated with me without words, letting me know she was okay and he wouldn't let anything happen to her. Besides he said Cee wouldn't let any of the guys push up on her. He knew her from high school. They were both seniors, only he was in college. I was so proud of my babies.

Cee had become a man, was strong and ready for something.

I wondered if he would go to the NFL now or wait for Sam. Without words, Sam told me that he would be pushing for Cee to go to the NFL when he graduated. He would help get him in. That would be great I thought. Now they needed to focus on next year and minimal injuries. When my daughter and Sam came home, they were tired. I had a nice dinner ready. Sam smiled and said he couldn't wait for us to live together. He said he was looking forward to our union and he appreciated me trusting him with my youngest daughter. She was special. I told him I knew that already. GOD was going to use her. He said he knew that also.

I realized I was getting closer to this man. He was physically and mentally attractive to me. He was so easy to love, maybe because he loved me, which made me comfortable and open to letting my guard down. I was going to enjoy getting to know Sam better than anyone else.

After dinner we had another long talk. No TV. We went in the back yard and pulled up chairs to the picnic table.

'Sam, how many others do I have to go thru before I can say we are dating exclusively?' I asked. 'Is this because of the females that showed their ass?' he asked. 'Yes! And the woman at your school; how many others, Sam?' He looked at me and smiled. 'What about all of your admirers, Fro? Do I need to get them straight or will you?' he asked.

I smiled too, thinking of a few men who were always asking me out. One man in particular was determined to win me over and he was sweet but it was too late. I was in love with Sam. Sam said, 'that's what I'm talking about also! That woman at school should have heard by now. Maybe word alone would make her back up. He said he wanted me to go to some of the school functions with him. They will be surprised but happy seeing my fine figure knowing that he was straight. He said that was a bad experience, he was glad it was over. Our final conclusion regarding our personal life was that we were dating exclusively and at this point we weren't sharing each other.

We both decided we would take our time and enjoy getting to know each other because it was no going back nor did we want to.

It wasn't going to be long before he would introduce me to his Dad and I would introduce him to my other children and my family.

We wanted to be comfortable with each other first. He reached over, kissed me on the side of my mouth then found my tongue, kissed it, then wrote on it, 'mine'. I got up, sat in his lap and kissed him passionately. He responded by holding onto my thigh and squeezing it, which tickled. He ran his other hand through my hair, which had grown a lot, and pulled me closer to him. I was totally enjoying this passion. I felt his little friend beneath me, rising. I moved around in response. He felt my breast and fondled my nipple through my shirt. He nibbled on it; I found his ear and did the same thing. We were so aroused. It had begun to get dark. We decided to get a quickie when Sam advised me that my daughter was asleep.

I got up from his lap and walked over to the tree. He watched me smiling.

I lifted my skirt a little to reveal the absence of panties. He walked over and unzipped his pants. I hugged the tree trunk and bent over a bit. Sam came up behind me and leaned in to kiss the back of my neck. He reached around, palmed my breast, gently squeezing then rolled my nipples between his fingers. I released a low moan. I felt his little friend between my legs. She was so wet she dripped on his little friend. He quickly found my soft spot and pushed inside. He had to open his legs wider to accommodate my height and to be able to get his little friend all the way inside. In this position, it was a totally tight fit. Sam blew on my ear and stuck his tongue in my ear. I felt electricity run through my body. I was wetter which made the fit juicier. Sam said, 'Baby this feels so good. I love sexing you up.' He pushed in more and told me to hold on to the tree. He found his rhythm and my spot at the same time. He didn't forget the cool down which felt great in the warm night air. He pulled out and turned me around. He picked me up and put his little friend inside.

I put my legs around his waist and he held me against the tree. He kissed my face and neck also. It really felt good being loved by this man. My man!
I held his face and kissed him passionately.

Team Prayer before Season
The next day would be the last day for football camp. There would be a scrimmage with one of the local colleges and then there was a luau party at the beach. Sam had already made arrangements. He was very good with planning events.
He said he wanted me to come pray with the team and ask for healing of their bodies and minds. He wanted the students to have fun playing ball and feel good too. After praying for guidance, I agreed. The next day I went out to the field just as practice was ending. Coach Sean and Frank smiled when they saw me approach Sam and hug him. Coach blew the whistle and asked everyone to gather over to us. He introduced me as his girlfriend. The players looked at my defined body and some said, 'damn Coach, she fine'.

He told them his assistant for the week was my daughter. They looked at her in surprise. Some of the team recognized me and asked Cee wasn't I the one who use to help him. I saw him shake his head saying yea! I heard another player say, 'don't let me find out Virginia Beach is where I should be visiting.' Sam stopped them and said, 'Quiet down now and listen. Fro has a real good relationship with GOD. HE answers her prayers. Look at me, she prayed for me and now I'm hers.' I hit him on his arm. They laughed. He said, 'No, on the serious tip, I asked her to pray for us and our up and coming year. We can use all the prayers we can get but Fro is special. Fro!' I spoke to all of them and thanked them for allowing me the opportunity to pray for and with them. I told them that I loved Sam and would not be letting him be without me any time soon. I obviously knew a lot about women, if any of them ever needed to talk in confidence, they could. I told them if they ever needed a hug or encouragement I was available for them.

I asked them not to allow young ladies and women to take advantage of them. Try hard to complete their degrees because there is life after football. They will need the education to continue being the leaders they already were. I asked them to hold hands and spread out in a small circle.

I shared with them my belief in Jesus, GOD and the Holy Spirit. If they believed in GOD this would still work.

I asked GOD to first forgive our sins and allow us a moment of HIS time. I said, 'We come to you humble Lord. We are but a grain of sand in this world but we belong to you. We are not waiting until something bad happens before we seek you. We seek you in good times too. We can't succeed alone GOD, we need you in our hearts and minds to keep us sane. We thank you for our past, no matter how bad or good. We thank you for our future and your part in it. We ask you to help us succeed in whatever we do and we especially ask you for favor. When it comes to our health, heal us GOD in Jesus name and make us whole. Heal our minds as well as our bodies.

We need both to survive. We ask you to heal our hearts too. Each of these, your children have something that needs to be whole or repaired. Heal our bodies so we can play in good health. This and all other silent prayers I ask and count it done, in Jesus name. Amen.'

As I prayed that prayer, I walked around the circle and touched each player's chest.

That last touch was Cee. He was standing next to Coach. Some of the players hugged each other with tears; others shook their heads up and down in confirmation. No one was untouched. They were good and so were the other coaches. Coach hugged me tight and thanked me for the prayer. He said without words that it was a success.

He asked my daughter if she wanted to go home with me or wait for him. She said, 'wait for him.' So I hugged Coaches Frank and Sean and left practice. My daughter and Sam were back at the house an hour or so later. They laughed as they came in the house. Dinner was light. We looked at a movie after showers. I have to say this was really nice. Love was intense tonight. It lasted on and off all night.

When I woke up the next morning, his little friend was guarding the soft spot entrance like a gate keeper. I had to laugh, which woke up Sam. He kissed me and his little friend pushed his way back into my soft spot. He found my spot right away and rubbed on it. Of course my body was at his command.

Sam finally got up and showered. He told my daughter she could sleep in and come to the scrimmage with me. She agreed. The game was on the Sports Center field.

We drove out there. We both wore shorts and sandals. It was hot at the beach. I wore my shades and hat. I was comfortable with using the tortoise tone as I called it. I have not had to use the regular anymore. I used the mild tone and lotion and used the conch oil when I was sore. I would be sharing some of these things with my daughter's like the shampoo and conditioner. They wouldn't need tortoise cream anytime soon. I chose not to discuss it at all for now. The existence of it would make folks lose they minds, do and pay any amount of whatever, for its use. The burden of knowing of it alone is hard.

What had Sam done, exposing me to the wonders of his world? There are things unnatural to the normal man. Why does Sam trust me so much? I'm struggling with how to hold this information. I guess I first see Nan and Poppy being exposed to multi-government investigations and claim. They are sweet, loving people that deserve only good in their lives. Besides they're Sam's Godparents and they love me. I love them too. Knowledge of tortoise cream would expose Jacob.

There would be no end to the agony it would cause Jacob and mostly Sam. I would never hurt them that way. I know what it means to ride or die. Taking a chance that Sam would keep the little friend away from me is certainly not an option. So here I am. My guard is totally down, almost. I'm not thinking of an exit strategy. This is certainly a priceless moment. I'm not going to share this information with anyone. Sam said without words, 'that's the woman I love.' No man or woman can penetrate the connection that GOD has allowed us to have.

The benefits of this relationship is also not a balanced measure but worth the ride. Our reward is being alive and having a real love relationship with everything on the table on both sides. On top of that, we're doing what GOD wants and as long as we do that, we are afforded the luxury of a complete love life. Wow, that's pretty deep when you think about it. We are on a real mission from The Father.

We finally found a parking space. I was beginning to think how convenient it would be to have someone save you a space or park your car. Now I knew how Sam felt when he valet his car or had special up front parking.

The scrimmage was free so no need for a will call. Sam said without words, that he needed a hug and kiss before he starts. He smiled when he caught my eye. So did I! Lord have mercy, this man was so fine. I could easily suck him up with a straw. I hugged him tight. We held each other for a moment. When I pushed back like I was done, he pulled me back and said, 'a kiss, too.' I smiled hard and said, 'I don't know you like that dude.' He pulled me to him and kissed me lightly on the lips.

He let me loose; I moved back from him and said in my mind, 'whose signifying now?' He smiled hard also.

It was fun watching the team because they were so funny. You could tell they felt great. They were honing skills and havin fun. It was hot so they would only do so much. Sam and I were noticed. If any dudes were interested, he killed that thought with our hug. The women watching knew they wouldn't have a shot because we are openly affectionate. We touch each other with familiarity of each other's body. There was no doubt we were dating.

He said, 'Baby, don't forget next week's meeting in Cozumel. You have to come.' I agreed to go. I would take the 3Seats design to check out mold and diecast options. I had access to the money it would take to get started so I would not waste time. This trip was for me too!

When the scrimmage was over, we hung around and waited for the team to get back on the bus. They had to go back to the hotel and change clothes.

The bus would drop them off at the beach party. I drove myself so I could leave when I wanted to.

There were a few faculty members there also. They smiled and spoke to me. When Sam came out to greet them he called me over and introduced everyone. He told them I was his woman. They said, 'okay Coach'. I laughed out loud. I told Sam to behave and go slow we are just beginning to date.

He said, 'okkkk'. His colleagues laughed also. The President of the college asked me was I coming to his staff cookout this year. It would be at his house, on campus. He said there's a pool out back, hot tub also. I asked if dogs got in the pool, he said no, only some of his dog friends with two legs. We all laughed. I told him if Sam invited me, I would come. Sam said, 'Fro, will you go to the cookout with me at the Presidents house with his pool and hot tub?' I said, 'of course I will.' I asked them if they were meeting us at the Luau. They said yes. Well this was gonna be interesting. Most people couldn't play Sam in a million years. Too bad they don't know that.

Sam said without words, 'People not gonna know what hit them. They already can't play you and you don't know what they think about you, before now. Knowing their agenda is half the battle.' Sam already had my back on that one. No more doing anything you want to my man. I believe I can hold my own. 'Sam they cut off from hurting you again. Those days are over,' I said. He said, 'Baby, You don't even have to tell um. Don't tell um.'

My daughter put out a tweet for cheerleaders from her high school, and two local colleges to come to the beach! The football team would have a lot of cheerleaders to socialize with. Being cheerleaders meant they were in similar physical condition. My daughter left with friends and would meet us by seven at the party.

Team Luau at the Beach
Sam came home with me to change. We got to the party as the others started arriving. The bus wasn't there yet with the players. Sam and I got a drink and found a spot to sit.

We talked about what he wanted me to do in Cozumel. He said it was a good idea to pitch 3Seats now. It's good to expect future business. Always a positive and gives people something to look forward to.

We kissed passionately a few times, and then mingled with the crowd. I stayed close to him as I had done in Cozumel at Sam's last meeting. I now know why he was teaching me this. It set a tone in a new circle of people. They know they can't divide or conquer us, together. This worked especially well with females. With gay men I came differently, I encouraged them to find someone else, cause they ain't gettin none of Sam Maxwell. His little friend has made its choice. He had to indeed win friends and influence people to do what he wanted.

The story moves on because Sam is capable of this very thing. He does it so well! The good thing for him is I am capable of the same. Even though the perks that came with Sam were mind blowing, I wasn't giving up me, to stuff that I could do without.

If he wanted to do things I wasn't free and willing to do he had to really convince me. Rules of engagement were no blatant disrespect or physical violence against me or my family. If this ever happened my family will come looking for him before the police is called. All of those wasted thoughts because our relationship is very, very good.

Speaking without words would be great for business. Some contracts would be ours out of curiosity of us. Those contracts had to be checked before agreement. Someone may want access to Sam for their own purpose. This was Sam's expertise. His seer ability was the advantage. He weeded out total users and did business with people who know how to or are determined to learn how to run a successful business. Wow, I was really feeling helping Sam in the future. If for no other reason, the fun! Another dip in the weird shower was an incentive to go to Cozumel also. Besides Carlo and I had unfinished business. Sam said without words, if you misbehave your punishment will be that shower. Remember what happened last time?

You know you can't run Fro. I can catch you.
All I could say was 'Stop playin boi.'
We made our way over to the President of the
college. He had a smile that said, 'Okay, let's
see what we have here.' Sam said without
words, 'You were exactly right. He wants to
know if this is short or long term. He also
wants to know how you slipped by him. He's
spent lots of time at the beach and local high
schools. Wow, he's even wondering what color
panties you have on, or if you have on any at
all!' It was hard looking at him knowing what
he thought of me. I almost laughed out loud
but Sam said without words, 'Baby, please be
good. This is my boss for a while longer. You
have an opportunity to have his friendship for
the rest of our lives. That's not a bad deal for
us. Remember your daughter will be attending
this college next year. This is a good setup
for her. She will be well taken care of.' I
stopped, stood up taller, pulled on Sam's arm
and grabbed his face.

I kissed him with tongue and expressed without words that I loved him a lot and loved him more for thinking about my daughter's well being. Please make an excuse to your colleagues. I let him go after a few moments. The President shook his head. Sam smiled at me and shook his head too. He said, 'I love you too baby.' The President chimed in and said, 'It is very romantic out here isn't it?'

I responded and said, 'I forgot we are with company. It's hard for me to pretend. I may calm down when we've dated longer.'

Sam said, 'I hope not because I like when you kiss me babe.' We all laughed. We moved on to speak with other friends and parents that were in attendance. They welcomed the attention Coach was giving them with his personal touch. He held my hand when he spoke with a woman or mom that had been attracted to him. A few of them I had seen before when I came to help Cee.

We turned around to the team getting off the bus and coming over to us. They were happy to see their folks and friends waiting for them.

They came straight over to Coach Max first and gave him pound before they dispersed around the campfire with their friends.

Coach finally whistled loud to get everyone's attention. He said he was trying something different this year. After he prayed over the food, he called my daughter to him.

She said the drinks are to the left but we have to have order so, ball players and staff, please grab two drinks for your parents or friends...then the cheerleaders will grab two drinks, one for you and one for ourselves...the food is on the right...do the same there.

Everyone shook their heads in agreement.

Sam and I grabbed three drinks in each hand and served the President and faculty. It was fun.

After we all ate as much as we wanted everyone broke off into small groups to enjoy the company of their family, friends and cheerleaders. My daughter asked the cheerleaders to perform a defense, offense and get the ball back cheer. We all laughed and had fun. The players don't get to see much cheering at da games.

At the conclusion, the President bowed his head to Sam in agreement.

When the caterer packed everything up, Sam went over to their truck and tipped them one hundred dollars each. They all smiled and a few hugged Sam.

After the team was back on the bus and the cheerleaders were gone, we left to go to my house. Sam packed his things and put his bag beside the door. We said good night to my daughter and went to bed. After individual showers, we laid in bed and both of us fell asleep in minutes. About 4 am I was awoken by his little friend inching his way deeper into my soft spot. He was beginning to increase in size and she was getting wet and excited. Sam turned me on my stomach and started the push pull movement until she got so wet it tickled him. He moaned in pleasure. I moved my behind up toward his little friend so he could go deeper. He brushed past my spot. I jerked up and down as I experienced a small tremor. Sam started kissing the back of my neck. It felt so good, I squirmed.

He massaged my breast in his hands and bit my ear. I rocked back and forth very slow. We spoke without words. He said he was so happy and pleased with his life right now. He loved making love to and with me. I could hardly breathe due to anticipation of his next move. He made my body respond at will to him and his little friend. Anything almost and anywhere is a good time for sex and love. I was not about to give this up. Ever!! He turned me over without taking his little friend all the way out. He found my ear and licked it. I let out a sound that he caught by covering my mouth with his. He held my legs open and snuggled inside. All of a sudden, he stopped. He smiled and kissed me with such passion, I felt faint. He pulled out enough to reposition himself to get my breast in his mouth. He sucked and licked with just the right amount of pressure. I came! His little friend grew harder. When he released my nipple, I relaxed more. He moved in and out fast about one minute, then moved in and out slow about one minute. He repeated this for about ten minutes.

I was constantly in an orgasm the entire time. He found my spot and rubbed it hard, then light. I know I passed out.

I felt myself coming back and feeling Sam making love to me so good I was cheering him on. After another few minutes, I felt Sam spray her. He had a weird look on his face. Then he smiled. He started the slow down movement that I loved. We kissed passionately for a few minutes before just holding each other while we fell back to sleep. Sam was up about 8am, showered and dressed for the ride back to Charlottesville. I went back to bed when he left. I slept about five more hours before getting up to the smell of grilled ham and cheese sandwiches. We were home safe and Sam made it home safe too.

Cozumel Visit/Business Changes

A week came fast and now I find myself at
the airport waiting for Sam to arrive. He flew
from Charlottesville to Newport News airport
to pick me up. I had my smallest suitcase and
a large purse. My children were texting me
with different issues. I had my back turned
from the terminal and deep into my response
when I heard Sam say, 'You ready?' He
touched my shoulder and I turned around. We
kissed and hugged. He grabbed my suitcase in
one hand and my hand with his other. We
walked towards a check point. Sam smiled at
the agent who waved us through. After
boarding and finding a seat, I heard Sam give
flight instructions over the radio.
We were stopping in Miami at Tami Ami
airport before going on to Cozumel. I was a
bit nervous but without words, Sam reminded
me to remember our promise of forty years. I
did and was able to relax. He invited me to
come into the cockpit with him but I refused.
I was not ready to see that far down yet.

When we arrived at Tami Ami, I got off the plane to stretch my legs. Sam went inside for a few minutes then we boarded again.

This time I sat in the cockpit. It was thrilling to take off and see the plane lift up into the sky. I know now why Sam felt the way he did about flying. Within two hours we were landing in Cozumel. Landing was a bit scarier. I held onto my chair arms. It was nice getting off in a hanger.

Sam took our bags and gave instruction to the hanger personnel that he needed to be refueled and he would be back to check in another day or so. He told them we would be leaving in three days. We walked out through a side door of the hanger. Carlo was waiting in his Hummer. He got out and greeted Sam with a handshake/half hug.

They spoke in Spanish but I heard it in English when Sam spoke. Sam said in Spanish to Carlo that he had to make it right with me. He said, 'She's aiming for you because of how you treated her when you first met. She's not gonna let it go, so you gotta come clean. She will know eventually anyway.'

I smiled and said, 'Yeah, whatever he said.' They looked at me and laughed out loud. Carlo walked over to me while Sam put our bags in the truck. Carlo grabbed my shoulders and pulled me to him.

He said, 'Hi woman.' I hugged him back and said, 'What's up dude.' He looked at me and said, 'We will talk.' I responded, 'We certainly will.' Sam got in the back seat of the truck. I smiled and shook my head. Carlo helped me into the passenger seat. We were at the house within fifteen minutes. Once in Sam's quarters I flopped down on the bed and looked at him. Without words, I asked him, 'What's the deal with Carlo.' He said Carlo doesn't know he is a Seer. He's never told him. Carlo is a little confused about his feelings for him. He has never come out and told Carlo that he knows what he thinks. He is happy that I am in his life now. He said Carlo is jealous of me. I told him thanks for sharing and that I would handle it at this point. He said Carlo is not gay, but confused with the bromance he has for Sam. He's known Carlo for more than ten years.

I told him I would not damage his relationship, but Carlo's position in Sam's love life would be made extremely clear. I was not sure of the tactic I would use yet but whichever one I used it would be gentle.

I wondered why Sam had not responded to my thoughts of being able to hear his Spanish as English. Sam came over and sat on the bed next to me.

He said without words that he knows I can hear his languages where I understand them. He went on to explain why he wanted me to come back with him. 'Currently, C&S has no US contracts. We chose not to because of my aspiration in the US with coaching football. However, I have known for years that we have not mined the silver nowhere near its capacity. The workers need more to do so they can make more money rather than just breaking even. Carlo is a very good manager/steward but lacks business skills in choosing business contracts. I've made minimal effort in teaching him because I've been busy watching my back especially with this women issue.

So many people thinking I'm gay or bi-sexual because I avoided most women. I am not telling them about my little friend. Now I don't have to at all. I knew this silver was being saved for a specific purpose but did not know what the purpose was before now. With your proposed order, it will inject more life here. (In HIS time)

Your order will be the first US contract. The workers need my input in the company also. They don't want to just deal with Carlo.

I can't be here as often as needed. That's where you come in again. Without words, we can discuss and multitask. My vision for the company can be realized and you can speak on my behalf, without me being present. I want to setup a retirement program for the employees. They've been asking for years. It would be an incentive for them. They saw you during the annual meeting and our interaction. They will trust you because I do. So you see, we need each other equally in this. I can trust you right, baby? This is My Mine, I purchased it legally. I share a third with Carlo because I can't be here as often as I'd like.

I have to trust him and make suggestions when I know he's having a hard time. I want to propose changing the financial structure. Profits will be divided four ways for a few years and then five ways permanently. Four ways is myself, Carlo, C&S and Retirement fund, five ways will include Charity and scholarships for the young people. Our business will work better if we think of and help others. I will share my profits with you. What do you think? I laid back down on the bed and looked up in the ceiling too stunned to laugh or make a joke.

My first verbal response was, 'My God! Where I am, you have to be there also. This is some ish…!' Sam said out loud to me, 'Fro, don't forget that, to whom much is given, much is required, even if you didn't ask for the assignment.' He had a point, I had to admit. I didn't look at Sam. I was trying to wrap my head around the fact that this is real. I looked over at the shower door. I could certainly use a warm shower and some love from Sam but he wanted an answer. We've only been dating officially for one month.

Am I ready for this? Sam is going to be more
visible now that he's dating me. 3Seats will
bring its own attention. GOD didn't say this
would be easy. Then again neither did Sam.
I love GOD with all my heart and I feel the
same about Sam, in our flesh. I got up on my
elbows and looked at Sam. He had his head
down. I said, 'Ok, I agree. I'll do it!' Sam let
out a deep breath. He pushed me over and
kissed me so deep, I almost lost my breath.
He kissed my cheeks and said, 'baby, you won't
regret this. I'm in love with you and I love you
for helping me. I promise I won't change on
you or leave you hanging.
I will help care for your baby girl too.' This
time I kissed him and hugged him tight and
said, 'You better!' He said he was tired and
needed to sleep. He looked drained. I told
him I will be back. I wanted to go for a swim
and catch Carlo to get something to eat.
I changed into a swim suit, checked myself in
a mirror and went downstairs. I didn't see
Carlo so I went outside to the pool.

It was very warm outside. I got in on the shallow end. After a few self dunks. I swam to the deep end and was proud of myself. I floated back to the area I could stand up in. I repeated the swim a few times.

Now tired, I sat on the steps in the shallow end. Carlo was sitting in a chair to my left. He was looking at me smiling. I threw water his way. He didn't move. I was hungrier than I was hot now. I turned to Carlo and really took a look at him. He was kind of fine. His hair is cut very neat but is straight with a few waves. His skin is caramel in color. He has facial features that reminded me of one of my cousins. He has large hands and arms. There was a sparkle near his face that reflected off the sun. He has a red diamond earring. He is indeed a man with substance. So you don't know how to feel about my Sam...well I do! I had to snap out of my internal conversation. 'Carlo I'm hungry. Did you cook?' He laughed out loud while shaking his head, no. 'I'm not cooking for you, Fro!' he said. 'Why you so mean to me?' I said as I stood up and got out of the water.

I walked straight over to him without a towel. He looked me up and down. I turned around and allowed him to see me from behind before turning back around. 'Can you take me to that place near Mimi shop so I can eat?' 'Let Sam take you.' 'I want you to take me, now. Sam is asleep. Can I drive back?' He smiled and asked if I was going to change clothes. I asked him if he thought I should or was he just embarrassed by me. I knew I wasn't twenty five or thirty years old anymore, but Sam loves me. He finally agreed to take me to eat. I found my shoes near the pool and walked back to the truck. This time he didn't help me get in. Oh! Dude was gonna pay for this behavior. I put my shades on. Then remembered I did not bring my purse. Carlo said I could pay him back. I asked him did he see the photos of me when Sam first took them. He said yes, he saw me himself. 'What was your impression?' 'You seemed like the kind of woman Sam would like to spend time with. He was right. But it is so soon for you to be so in love.

He gave you his company profits after eight days of spending time.' 'So, you mad about that? Carlo I didn't know about a company, any meetings or money before I came here with Sam. I didn't ask him for it, he pushed it on me. He doesn't care about money as much as he does about me. He can get more money but he can't get another me. You his boi and partner. He loves you but you can't satisfy his hunger for me. No one can! But me! I love him Carlo. Does Sam have another woman you'd prefer him to be with?' He said, 'No'. 'I'm not with Sam for money. He needs me too. I know you know about that Coach thing and how they are now backing Sam. I'm not going to allow anyone to take advantage of him and ain't nobody, male or female ever gonna get Sam again. We totally satisfy each other and that has never happened to either of us before. There's no going back now. I'm it!' Carlo looked me up and down and said, 'I bet.' 'Carlo we are gonna have to work together so you might as well be nice to me. I'm not a bad person.

If you allow it, you will see I'm just me, I can't pretend long.' Just then we pulled up at the Taco stand. I got out. I ordered chicken tacos and plantains. Carlo paid and gave me the receipt. I snatched it and licked my tongue. He shook his head and laughed. I asked him if Mimi had brought any material to him, he said no. I asked if I could get the truck key. As soon as he gave me the key I started to run and talk at the same time saying I was gonna go to Mimi's. He ran to me and caught me before I crossed the street. He picked me up from behind and carried me back to the taco stand while I kept saying put me down. I have to say I felt protected in his grip. For a moment I imagined him with Sandy. After I got my food, I put it in the truck and started getting into the drivers seat. Carlo caught me by my waist and pulled me from the truck. His grip on me spoke volumes. He liked the way I felt, I could tell. He said he wants to drive. I told him to stop handling me before I hit back. He laughed and let me go when he was near the passenger door. I knew at that moment, I had broken through his ice.

It was only a matter of time now. I had almost forgotten that I had red streaks in my hair and average body fat. He was attracted to my body. Sam said to me without words, 'He can want you all he wants to but you are my woman, not his. Stop teasing him Fro, come home.' I told Carlo that Sam should be up by now. He agreed and drove us back home. Sam was sitting on the deck in the shade, when we pulled up. I was almost finished eating when we got out of the truck. I gave Sam the last bite and sat in his lap. He held me. He looked at Carlo while he rubbed my thigh and said, 'I know you know she's beautiful, but she's my woman and I won't share her.'

I laughed and said stop being so possessive, Carlo don't like me like that, as a matter of fact, he has been being mean to me. Tell him I'm good people baby. He doesn't believe me. Sam smiled and asked Carlo, 'You know she's special right? You also know, I really care about her?' Carlo said, 'Yeah, okay, I get it.' Sam told Carlo I would be coming back occasionally to help and would be staying here.

'Don't let anything happen to her, please.'
Carlo said, 'I got you man.' I said without
words, 'You go baby you hit him high, I'll hit
him low. That combo works. Sam responded
that Carlo would still try me because I was a
woman. He said he wasn't sure if me using my
feminine influence would break Carlo. I said
we will see. Sam responded, 'He's a man, Fro!
He can handle most women, even you.' I
reminded Sam that he has introduced Carlo to
Sandy and he travels to the states. Maybe
Carlo needs a healing. Sam laughed out loud.
Sam had food delivered for dinner. We all sat
around and discussed the business.
I told Carlo about 3 Seats and my desire to pay
to have it made here. Carlo seemed excited.
Sam said without words, 'Told you so! The
workers will be encouraged also. No more
hiding, Fro.' I asked Carlo who was the mold
maker. He said it depends on the security for
the product. He suggested I have high
security which meant he would be doing the
work on the mold himself. Once he has the
original he will determine how many can make
up a diecast.

I will decide on sizes and purchase cases for the diecast plate to be stored in. Carlo told me that was a part of the price because Mimi made the cases they used. I totally agreed. He asked me how long had this idea been simmering. I explained that it's been ten years or more. I had a few of the seats created.

But the price of gold went up seems like overnight. I could not afford to produce anymore. Using silver seemed like settling for less of GOD. The message however would not die. Until recently, I thought all this information inside me was a part of my imagination. I was ready to be without a partner for the remainder of my life, stepping in and out of my self-made pity parties. I looked at Sam and said, 'I never thought I would meet this man. He's different for sure but I know without question that he loves me.' Sam said, 'Amen!' I reached over and kissed his lips very lightly. Carlo just looked at us and smiled. He said, 'How much do you plan to spend initially, Fro?' I looked at Sam who said without words, 'A million.' I repeated what he said. Carlo laughed. We all laughed. Carlo said, 'So you spending your money on this project?' I said, 'what money? What project? No one must know in advance or at all until it's time.' He said he understood. Sam spoke up and caught Carlo by the shoulder. He told us that he trusted Carlo.

Who is ride or die, while looking at Carlo. Carlo responded, 'That's what's up!'

Sam went on to explain to Carlo about his desire to create a retirement account. He also explained that they should not profit less because of the added business. He would explain at the quarterly meeting with the employees. There won't be money available until the end of the fiscal year. He asked Carlo if he objected to me coming back a few times to help set it up. He told him he would be busy with the team til early spring.

He also included that I would be under his direction. Carlo agreed saying he did not want to do that much paperwork anyway. He preferred the creative side and day to day activities. Sam said, 'Ok that's settled. Fro will be staying in my quarters when she comes for visits so can I ask you to look out for her, Carlo?' Carlo responded, 'Yes, I will watch her.' Sam looked at me shaking my head sideways with my head down, smiling. He turned to Carlo who was smiling also looking at me. He must have heard Carlo thinking about how he wanted to watch me.

He said without words that I must have forgotten I had red streaks in beautiful hair and that fine body spoke without words.

He said Carlo has not forgotten and enjoys every minute of his view. I said, 'Baby you not jealous are you?' He said I should be careful because my body and aura may be seen before I spoke. I may have to defend myself. I told him I defend myself well even with him. He laughed out loud. He told Carlo not to forget that I was his woman and he had plans for my future. Carlo responded. 'Um huh,' while looking at me. I got up and walked past Carlo over to Sam, sat beside him and kissed his lips very slow. He could only respond the same. I told him without words that I needed him to touch me all over, alone. He said, 'Yes baby, me too.' We both got up and walked toward the stairs. Sam turned to Carlo and said, 'My woman.' Carlo laughed out loud. We walked upstairs to Sam's quarters. We both yelled good night to Carlo at the same time, without a response. Sam grabbed my waist and pulled me to him. He kissed me very light on my lips, face and neck.

He reached down and started undressing me. He undressed and caressed me at the same time. There was electricity felt between us. His touch was gentle and firm. He moved back to look at my naked body, when he did, I reached over, ran my hands under his t-shirt to his chest. I pushed his t-shirt up and over his head. I ran my fingers thru his chest hairs and down his stomach to his pants. I bent over and pulled them down. His little friend was waiting for me. It moved as it got harder. I rubbed it and squeezed with light touches. Sam stepped out of his pants and underwear.

He reached for my hand and led me to the bathroom and the cylinder shower area. We both got in the hot tub. The bubbling water felt so good on my body. I could feel my muscles relaxing. I looked at him with a look that said I want you! He put his legs on each side of me and squeezed. He motioned with his arms held out for me to come to him. I did! He held me in an embrace that said I care about you.

We kissed long and passionately. Our tongues danced together before he held mine and wrote, 'I got you.' I totally relaxed in his arms while he rubbed my back and hips. His little friend found the opening of my soft spot and pushed his way in. I repositioned myself to allow him to fill me more. I laid my head on Sam's shoulder and held him around the neck in response to his movements. He pulled me close which made his little friend go deeper. I jumped when he brushed my spot but Sam held me tight enough that he absorbed the jolt too. He moaned. I kissed his neck and sucked his ear lobe then whispered in his ear. 'I'm in love with you Sam; no one else can change my mind about you. I'm yours baby because I want to be, as much as you want me to be.'

He responded by pushing my hips down to totally take all of him. He paused in place. We were connected at that moment. I released his neck and leaned back to look in his face. A tear began to fall down his cheek, he had his eyes closed.

He told me he was scared this day would never come. I stood up slowly releasing his little friend. He opened his eyes and smiled at me. I stepped out of the hot tub and turned on the rain forest shower head. I stood under it and allowed the water to wash the bubbles off.

Sam was watching me and still smiling. He got out of the hot tub and joined me in the shower. I quickly moved away and grabbed a towel. Kept thinking about the last time we were here. Sam heard my thoughts and said without words that I was being good so he wouldn't do it. I responded that I was sure I could think of or do something by tomorrow. We went back to the bedroom area and dried each other.

His little friend had a good time stroking me and bringing me to multiple climaxes. There were no words spoken, just satisfying noises. Our flesh was thoroughly satisfied and we slept in each other's arms almost all night. The next morning we had a second round even with morning breath the love making was great.

There was no way either of us would release the other. The sex alone was too good.

We showered together to save time and dressed in business casual clothing for the meeting at C&S Mining. The weather was very warm. Sam wore a dark tan leisure suit with a cream button down shirt. He looked like a boss and acted the same. I wore a white rayon skirt and a coral top. The multi-colored, coral, three inch wedges were perfect. I wore a ponytail hair style. Carlo had already gone to the office. We grabbed a snack before leaving for the meeting.

The employee's seemed happy to see Sam and I. Sam spoke in Spanish. I understood everything he said but, in English. He received a standing ovation at the end. He told them that I would be back a few times without him. He made them laugh when he said he expected them to treat me well and help me if I needed it, but don't run me away. I hit him on the arm, saying stop it. After the meeting, Sam took me to see Mimi. She had the purple fur with a paisley pattern in it. It was so nice, tears filled my eyes.

I told her I wanted a long skirt and jacket. She measured me and said okay. She said she would make the lining a nice pattern and a top too. I hugged her. She held me tight and said Jacob. I smiled and said yes. She said she was working on an outfit Jacob had her making for me. I told her I would be back in a month. Sam took me for a ride to a nearby town. We had dinner and enjoyed each other's company for a few hours.

When we got back, Carlo asked Sam to go to a party with him, alone. I was good and didn't want to go even if asked. I stayed at the house, smoked a joint and took advantage of the hot tub.

The next morning we got up and spent time with Carlo before he took us back to the airport. The plane was ready. Sam went thru all the checks before we left. I have to say, he's a very good pilot. We arrived at Tami Ami airport where Tortuga warehouse was located. After refueling, we left for VA. Sam walked me to my car. I was back at home within thirty minutes.

President's Cookout

The next day Sam told me the college president cookout was next week. He asked me to come and go with him. I'd be staying at his house. My daughter was still visiting relatives. School would be starting soon and my time would be limited. It almost seems like I'm on a train ride. Sometimes it doesn't stop. It felt good to be home and alone for awhile. Sam said without words that he knows how I feel. For a few moments I forgot he could hear my thoughts.

I guess this means here on earth, I'm actually never alone. Sam said, 'exactly.' It was suggested he doesn't have to answer all the time, some thoughts should be my own without response. He said he would but he was getting use to this too. GOD was probably laughing at us. Sam was preparing the team for their season while I spent the week researching retirement plans and contracts associated with them.

I prepared and refreshed myself with the original 3Seats plan. I would take the original mold back with me to Cozumel.

It was actually exciting to know this assignment would be completed sooner than later. The fact that I was a millionaire had not sunk in yet. There were a lot of people I was going to bless. I would start with my closest friends. Sam said without words to be extremely careful and selective. I assured him I would. For example I would help my friends who have a small business. They can put the money in a safe deposit box and plan for a year or so out. The money could be assumed savings, saved overtime. No one would question it. Sam said that's my girl.

I told him he was a great teacher, by the way, thanks for the money he made from business profits last year. He told me he loved me.

I was happily busy for the rest of the week. Sam was having fun, at last, with the team and staff.

The weekend was here and time to travel to UVA to see my man and his boss with friends. It was now mid-summer and hot. My hair was fierce. I wore beach clothes and took a dress for a possible outing.

Sam said he was hungry for me so outings would be limited. I left late Friday for the two hour drive. Sam spoke to me without words most of the way. It was becoming more comfortable using this form of communication. We knew it was only a matter of time before I mastered this technique. When I arrived, Sam was standing in the driveway waiting for me. We grabbed my things and went inside. This was my first visit to his home at UVA. There were hardwood floors and teakwood all over. He said it reminded him of Jamaica and his house there. The décor was leather and blinds to all windows. There were a lot of items like pillows, etc in school colors and logo. He said students and staff gave them to him over the years. The kitchen was nice with stainless steel appliances and an electric stove with microwave above it. There was a small, tall table with four chairs. I saw a deck off the kitchen. There was a bedroom in the back with bathroom attached. We went up a few stairs to an open large room. It was awesome. So it turns out the house was a small split level.

Sam had a king bed with TV mounted on a wall. There was a love seat next to a window that looked out toward the campus. There was a small desk with laptop in the corner. The bathroom was large and reminded me of Nan's. It had a separate shower with clear walls and spa, deep tub. There were double sinks and the toilet was in a corner separated by walls. He had a walk-in closet that was half full. He put my bag down beside the love seat. I fell into the bed. I was kind of tired from the drive. He asked was I hungry. I said yes but only needed a small dinner. He said he had not cooked anything and had a perfect place in mind to take me. We went to a jazz bar that you didn't have to dress up and shared a chicken salad.

They had baked chicken and it had a great taste. We were noticed by many. I smiled and told Sam without words that I sure don't feel like running into any of his old flames tonight. He said the past will stay in the past and we are here now. He reached over and pulled my ponytail. We went back to his house, showered and went to bed.

He said we had a long day tomorrow. There were places he wanted to show me, before the cookout. He wanted to get a haircut and stop by and see Sandy. I wanted to see her too.

Hot Love

He held me, rubbed my breast and behind for awhile. We kissed passionately. We really missed each other. He knew when he felt my soft spot, it was nice and wet. She was ready for her little friend and he was ready for her because I felt him moving against my leg. This was my first time at Sam's house. The love making would have to be memorable. Sam said without words that he has been waiting for this day. I told him I was excited to be here and I brought the conch oil just in case. He said Nan was exceptionally, special. He was glad she was his Godmother. I agreed. He told me to relax and allow him to love me right. I said okay. It was so nice not to have to think of masturbating anymore. Sam could bring me to multiple orgasms.

He asked if he could do what he wanted, the way he wanted to tonight and it would be my turn tomorrow. I agreed. He kissed my stomach and went down to kiss my soft spot. It was so wet. He started licking all the wetness and swallowing it. He blew my soft spot lightly. I moaned lightly. He proceeded to kiss it like he did my lips. It felt so good I relaxed and enjoyed the ride. His tongue lightly moved around the opening of my vagina then moved inside as far as it would go. The muscles opened and closed around his tongue. His tongue curled and went flat inside my vagina which caused a strange sensation. It made me push my hips up to feel it better. Sam held my hips up and put his thumbs on each side of my anus which made me squirm. He knew I didn't want anal sex, his thumbs didn't touch my anus but the sensation of almost, was overwhelming. I trusted Sam and allowed him to sex me up. He licked and sucked and kissed my soft spot until I came.

The position of his thumbs added another sensation that was like nothing I ever felt before. I could only squirm, rub his head and say, 'Oh baby.' After about five minutes of this, he moved up and his little friend dragged past my anus that he was still holding between his thumbs. I screamed with pleasure. His little friend entered my soft spot and Sam moved his hands to my hips and then my thighs. He pushed further in and touched my spot. I had a mini tremor. When the base of his penis was touching my soft spot, I felt so full and warm. I could feel his little friend pulsating inside me, although Sam was still. I could feel his penis growing harder and harder. Now it was pressing on my spot which triggered an auto orgasm. Sam started moving in and out without totally withdrawing. I was moving with him at the same pace. The feeling was so good I almost passed out. I started crying and asking Sam why was he doing this to me. He didn't answer me. After about ten minutes he started rubbing on my spot. I had a nonstop orgasm.

He moved out so the head of his penis was touching and rubbing my spot. All of a sudden he stopped with the head still on my spot. It sucked my spot which sent me to another level. I started screaming and crying while having an orgasm at the same time. Sam reached down and sucked my breast. My mind blanked out for a moment. I came back to myself and Sam kissing my lips softly, but I was still having an orgasm. My legs couldn't move and Sam was having an orgasm too. I felt the spray on my spot. He pulled out without taking the head out and repositioned me on my stomach. He pushed in from the back and held my hips up so I was on my knees. He pushed in and out fast, then slow. After a few minutes I was screaming again with a full orgasm. Sam had another one at the same time. He moaned loudly and said he loved me and was so in love it almost hurt. I knew exactly what he meant. We slowed down and he moved slowly until we both caught our breath. His little friend got softer and he pulled him out. I felt the head pop out. We were both so wet and so was the sheet.

After a few more minutes I got up to pee and Sam got a towel to cover the wetness in the bed. When we went back to bed, I asked Sam what was that for. He said he has never made love in this house or ever like that. He said, 'Fro, you belong with me. I know I can love you right and you certainly are receptive to me. I'm in love with you woman and I know you love me, don't you?' I could only tell the truth which was, yes! 'Yes baby, I'm in love with you too.' The love making was great and I slept very well.

Sam was already up when I woke up. I felt myself, I was pretty sore. Good thing I brought the conch oil. Sam said without words that it may not be a good idea to use it right now. I told him he should have thought about that before he had his way with me.

After we got dressed, we left the house and went by Sandy's shop. It was so nice seeing her. She was thrilled with my hair and was happy when I asked her for a cut. Sam waited a few minutes before he went next door to get his hair cut. The other ladies in the shop noticed Sam right away.

He said without words that they were thinking of what they could do to him but wondered if they'd have to deal with me. I told Sandy, loud enough for everyone to hear me, that I hope word is out that Sam has a girlfriend, cause ain't nobody got time to be cussing other women over a man. Sam laughed and said, 'Baby, you are my lady and nobody else, there's no need for cussing.' Sandy said she agreed with Sam. We finally left and went over to the president's house. His name is David Blusteen. The house is very large for a man with no children. But he probably entertains a lot. Sam said it was part of his job to host affairs for the college when other college presidents and people on that level, came to visit. He said he has to do the same sometimes as a head coach. Sam pulled in front on the end so he could easily get out. There were a few cars already there. We wore swim gear. I had on a shirt and shorts over my bathing suit. Mr. Blusteen greeted us from the side of the house before we got to the door. He shook Sam's hand and hugged me saying thanks for coming.

Sam said without words that he likes me and couldn't wait to see me in the pool. Remember to stay close to me just like before. We held hands as we entered the back yard. There were about twenty people there already. They noticed us right away. Mr. Blusteen introduced us as head Football Coach Max and his lady Fro. I waved to everyone. We spoke with the president for a few then went to get food and drinks. We didn't have breakfast. The food was catered and pretty good. We both had Dos Equis beer. After we ate, Sam caught my hand and began to walk around introducing us to the people gathered. Sam said without words that they wondered how we met. He said most thought we were a nice couple. They knew we were intimate because of how we touched.

Towels were already near the pool so we put our things on two chairs and got in. Sam dunked me, I screamed. He pulled me underwater and kissed me, before bringing me back up. I swam to the shallow end. Sam went the other way. The president got in the water so did a few others.

He wanted to play volley ball or something like it. If you dropped the ball in the water you were out.

In the end Sam won. I swam out to him. We rubbed and kissed each other while they watched. We got out on the shallow end. All eyes were on us. I didn't care because I knew who I was leaving with and the homies weren't gonna touch this. Sam laughed at me. After another two hours of laughing, talking and playing, we left. Mr. Blusteen said he was happy for us, wished us well and a successful season. Sam and I thanked him.

We went to Sam's house for more fun without an audience. I was hungry for this man, day love was great. We slept for hours afterwards. Sam made it clear that he wanted me to come to as many games as possible. I promised I would.

He understood my youngest was a high school senior and had a schedule too. My schedule was full this year but it was fine.

My Calling

It was the middle of September. My daughter had started her senior year. My schedule was beginning to get busy. Without words Sam reminded me I needed to go to the Caribbean to oversee some business. I agreed. I enlisted a family friend to stay with my daughter for a four night five day extended weekend while I was away on business. I gave her money even though she agreed to help without payment.

Sam had trained me and would be walking me through the process without words. I would be flying on Sam's jet with a pilot he knew. Cozumel was my first stop. Carlo picked me up from the airport. We had a short meeting at C&S regarding the mold for 3Seats. I left the

original mold with him.

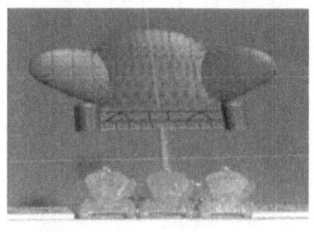

The security was high so he handled everything himself. He let me drive his Hummer to pick up my outfit from Mimi that Jacob had her make for me. This is the second one of his designs.

She was happy to see me and I her. She finished the fur outfit. It was hanging in the back of the shop. When I saw it, the tears started to flow. It was gorgeous. She took it down for a closer look. It felt wonderfully soft. The lining and matching shirt had the eternal love symbol on it and was so hot. The shirt accentuated my breast. It had three quarter sleeves and the purple fur was only in the front center. I tried it on and checked myself in the mirror. It fit perfectly. I already had boots that would match it. Mimi hugged me before I could hug her. Even she loved it on me. Before I took it off, she walked away to a back room and came back with a garment bag. She gave it to me and put a few tissues in my hand. I sat down in a chair because I didn't know what to expect. When I unzipped the bag, I put my hands to my mouth.

Sam said without words that Mimi was thinking there is no way she would have thought of a design like this and was so proud to help Jacob by putting it together for me. She knew this was bigger than us and was proud to be a part of it. I asked Sam how long and why was all of this bottled up in Jacob. He told me to ask Jacob myself. He would not answer me. I reached for Mimi and hugged her tight. I thanked her and kissed all over her face. She smiled and acted like it tickled her. We both laughed. I zipped the bag back up without trying it on. She said she knew it would fit.

So did I. After changing out of the fur outfit, I went back to the house. Still stunned, I found a Cozumel joint and sat on the back deck to smoke. Sam spoke with me without words and said Jacob loved me.

After a few puff puff no passes, I was more calmed. I smiled to myself thinking this is something else. There is no limit to what My GOD can do nor the beauty HE allows us to see. No one would believe Jacob designed clothing like this. I would love to see him in action. Maybe I will get the chance tomorrow.

I better say my prayers tonight. Sam said without words that I can't die for forty years.

I told him he was wrong for saying that. We both laughed.

Carlo called me to come pick him up from work. We stopped for dinner before going home. Carlo talked with me briefly about 3Seats. He seemed to understand what I'm looking for.

I retired to Sam's quarters. Everything I needed was there, especially the hot tub.

The next morning Carlo took me to the airport. We left for the short trip to Jamaica. Michael was waiting for me. He was all smiles and gave me a big hug. He said, 'you know I don't rise this early on the weekend woman'. I thanked him for coming to get me. He took me to Sam's house and took my bags inside. He said I should use the Jeep. We passed S&M on the way to the house. Michael said he would catch up with me later.

I looked around the house again with only my eyes. It was really cozy. I could see myself spending time there. I looked around outside. It was still early morning.

I went out on the porch after making my

Special coffee which consisted of **Tortuga Rum Cream coffee, brewed with bottled water, vanilla caramel creamer, sugar-in-the-raw** and **Hershey's chocolate caramel mini creamer. This combination should be illegal.**

The outside view was awesome. There was lots of greenery everywhere. Blue water was on the horizon. Sam said without words that this is a very special view that he often misses. I understood what he meant.

Saturday morning in Jamaica with good weather and ability to drive Sam's Jeep was so awesome. The garment bag with Jacob's outfit was placed in the back seat. We will both see this at the same time. First, there were buyers coming to the office this morning to discuss quantity, price and delivery times for subsequent orders. Sam knew what he wanted to do based on his discussions with Michael and the staff. He would be speaking to me without words during the meeting. Michael will advise that I am in attendance on Sam's behalf and I will make the final decision. This is going to be a trip but no turning back now.

Caribbean Flow

I changed into business casual clothing and left the house in the Jeep. The company was not far away. I pulled in the first available parking and got out. Sam's parking fetish was rubbing off on me. Michael laughed when he saw Sam's Jeep in the front parking space. He asked if Sam told me to do that. I laughed and said no, but I laughed when he brought me there for the first time and took that first parking space.

The first buyers were brought into the conference room by the front desk assistant. Two gentlemen dressed in leisure suits came in, Michael asked them to sit. They owned a cruise line that had never purchased from S&M before. Michael gave them the company history and advised them of other cruise lines that have expired or current contracts. They both pulled out their magnifying glasses to look at samples of the precious stones and diamonds. Once they chose what they wanted and the quantity, Michael plugged in the numbers on his laptop and printed the estimate sheet. The buyer brought cash to finalize their purchase.

They also had cashier checks for supplemental, smaller orders that will be shipped to them in a month. I looked over the paperwork, took the money and prepared receipts for all orders. Michael had the initial orders prepared right away as the buyers would be taking the order with them. The men gave me very warm smiles. Sam said without words that they were wondering if they could have a threesome with me tonight in Jamaica. I quickly expressed our appreciation for their business. They were advised that Sam will be following up with them to make sure they were well treated and are satisfied with their purchase. They didn't ask me any personal questions.

About an hour later, a Representative from a UK company that sells jewelry online comes in. It's a woman and a man. They were dressed very stylish. They wanted unique pieces, some loose precious stones and diamonds in different colors. They too had cash for their purchase and preordered using a cashier check for an additional order in a month that could be shipped or carrier delivered. We had snacks that included Tortuga cakes, candy and coffee.

There was even a platter of mild jerk pulled BBQ. The buyers were given Tortuga brochures with their receipts. Their initial orders were prepared for them to carry with them. They seemed happy with the transaction. There were no more meetings today.

I took the garment bag to the back room where Jacob was. He appeared to be waiting for me. I smiled as I walked over to him and grabbed his hands. He smiled and felt up my arms to my face. He felt my hair then pulled me closer for a hug. He was very gentle with me. I told him that I wanted to try on the dress for the first time in his presence so we can see each other's reaction. He laughed and said okay. I grabbed the garment bag and gently took out the outfit. It was a butter amber colored sweater dress that came above my knees. The pattern embedded into the sweater was the eternal love symbol. There was short haired, butter amber colored fur at the hem, the waist like a belt, just above the breast, on the top of the back, the shoulder straps and suspension three quarter sleeves.

It had a hidden zipper on the side. I took my clothes off without regard to Jacob since he was blind. I put the dress on. It fit perfectly and it was soft. I found a mirror and took a look. I could only laugh out loud. Jacob asked what I was laughing for. I told him he was something else. He asked if I like it. I walked over to allow him to feel it on me. He felt the sweater on my body from top to bottom. I watched him feel for any imperfections. He then felt the position of the fur. It tickled when he felt it across my breast. He said Mimi did a perfect job on this one. She stitched it exactly how he requested it. He smiled and said, 'I think you look hot in this dress. I know it has to feel good. Not too hot or cold.' I told him it was so awesome and I am so proud of him. He said, 'Thank you, Fro!' A promise was made to wear the dress when Sam and I went out. Photos will be taken of it too. He told me he had two more outfits in mind but wasn't sure of the details yet.

Knowing the chance being taken, did not stop me from asking Jacob could we have dinner tonight. He said yes. I asked what he liked to eat and from where.

I would pick it up and he can come to Sam's house when it was time. He seemed surprised that I asked. Sam said without words that he is. He thought you would be too afraid to be alone with him without me being present. This is your chance to ask him whatever you want and get an honest answer. My response was; my chance! I had the food delivered so there was time for me to take a shower and change clothes before dinner. The dinner was good. Jacob and I sat around listening to music and talked. There were a few tears shed with some of his responses. I asked him how he felt as a child and when his mom died. I also asked about him and Sam. I went all the way there. 'So Jacob do you believe in and have a relationship with GOD?' His response made me cry. 'Woman you are something else. I knew you would ask. We been waitin for you, longtime. Sammie and me just knew you had to be somewhere. If GOD made us then HE could make you too. We asked for perfect love with someone we could touch while we here on dis earth. Sammie asked for real love when you don't have to speak out loud. He wanted a woman he could feel her energy and they would be inseparable. That's you, Fro.

I asked for a woman who was sent by HIM to have mercy on me and not judge me cause what I look like. It's not my fault Fro. Is that woman you, too?' It was so touching and confusing. I would pray about it and get back with him. My turn was up; told him about me, how I grew up, my children and some of my family. He was reminded of all the miraculous things I've been exposed to and how **it had me worried about my safety** until I realized Sam and I are being allowed a complete love because we listen and do what GOD ask us. It feels like we are on a real mission from HIM! He responded; you are!

I slept in Sam's bed with the island radio station on all night. Sam and I talked dirty for awhile, without words.

The next day was Sunday. I was carrying several million dollars from buyer purchases that needed to be deposited into the S&M business account which was in the Caymans. The bank wasn't opened until Monday. I stayed in Jamaica one more night and spent time with Michael. He wanted to teach me a few words in his dialect. We rode around town for an hour or so making Michael's women mad.

They didn't know who I was. I did see Monie standing at a fast food place. She knew who I was and called me by name. I yelled back, 'What's up womon!' She laughed and told me I was crazie. We both laughed out loud.

Michael took me to one of Jacob's houses. He had more than one or two. He was more relaxed lying on his side but then again so was I. There was another couch nearby. I laid down on it to talk with Michael and Jacob. Sam said without words that he was proud of his family for not pouncing on my fine ass. I laughed out loud and so did Jacob. He heard what Sam said too.

Michael wanted to go over the upcoming orders that had to be processed in a month.

I left Monday morning for the Caymans and went straight to the bank. The lady there remembered me from before. After the business was completed the rest of Monday was spent with Nan and Poppy. They shared their own business strategies and family history with me. It was a loving afternoon.

Tuesday morning I was back at home. I needed to be home before my daughter got home from school.

Thanksgiving Football with the Family

The team was undefeated when winter break approached. I had gone to many football games, college and high school, in the past 3 months. Sam and I talked a lot.

It was time to meet our other part of the family. I had not met Sam's dad even though he came to a game that I just happened to miss. My adult children knew I had a boyfriend and he was UVA Football Coach but had not made it to a game yet. They supported my youngest high school events. We invited our immediate family to the game before Thanksgiving. I cooked at Sam's house. My adult children were given tickets to the game and a VISA card with enough money on it to get gas and a hotel room. Sam's dad and my mother would also have hotel rooms close to the house. They all came. It was so nice. I never told my family that Sam was a seer. He said his dad didn't know either. I was the only one outside of the islands who knew. He finally told me that besides Jacob, Michael and his Godmother Nan, no one else knew.

After the game everyone came over to Sam's. It was so nice meeting his dad. He was a tall 6ft man with curly grey hair. His eyes were gray and he was a little muscular. He had large hands and feet. He was handsome and carried himself with confidence. He hugged me and said he was happy Sam found me because he was unhappy for so long. He told my mom that she had a lovely daughter, while hugging her, too. I introduced him to my children. His name is Sean Maxwell. He doesn't look like he is all white.

I can see where Sam gets some of his good looks from even though he is much darker than his dad. I turned on some music and started warming up the food. Sam and I had already put any valuables away so I told them to go ahead and look around. Sam came in and I introduced him to my older children. He hugged them and said, 'welcome.' He said without words that they wondered what he wanted with me. They hoped I wouldn't get attached to Sam because they believed he would hurt me, he could have any woman he wanted.

He said, 'Baby they don't know or understand.'
I agreed. We all ate, talked and laughed.
Several of the grandchildren were there too.

Sam, the older children and son in law went
out on da deck to smoke. My mom and Mr.
Maxwell talked about things of their
generation. The kids played with Sam's
stuffed school items and the others were on
their cells. When we were all together again,
Sam spoke and explained how he felt about me
and that no one was gonna come between us,
but he wanted their love and respect and was
willing to give the same. The smaller children
said, 'Okay Sam!' My youngest said she was
already down and knew Sam loved me. Sam
said without words, 'That's my girl. She misses
her dad, but knows you're happy with me. She
feels safe with me!' My son spoke up and said
he didn't need another father but was willing
to be friends. How good a friend would depend
on Sam. My oldest daughter and her husband
agreed. My mom said she felt good about Sam
and me. His dad co signed. Sam said our
parents hit it off, maybe a little too much. I
laughed out loud.

I said, 'We are mature enough to make our own decision about our relationship but are choosing to include you all like we have to get your buy in, sounds silly to me.'

My son said its good that Sam wants to include us besides I need a man around with all ya'll women. My son in law co signed. I shook my head. Sam chimed in that soon he wanted all of us to cruise with stops in the Caribbean. He said he wanted all the grandchildren to go too. He told them he would pay for the trip. Sean asked could he come too. Sam said of course. My mom smiled. Sam was arranging what she asked for, spending time with her grand's and great grand's. His dad said, 'Finally some family who loves my son. I'm so happy.' I told his dad that whether the children faded away or not, I was never leaving Sam. Sean started to cry. Just as Sam was about to console him, my mom hugged him. He hugged her back. We all looked at each other and busted out laughing. My mom tried to tell us that wasn't nice and to stop but she was not aware we were laughing at her too. Sam said without words, 'Here we go!'

I responded without words that he wanted them all to meet so this is what you get. He hugged me, too. It was a nice day and evening. We talked for awhile longer then our parents left first. They were staying at the same hotel. My older children left next, leaving the younger children with us at the house. The children took the downstairs bedroom. They all slept together. Sam and I went upstairs. After showers, we talked and cuddled for awhile before sleep took over. The next morning I fixed breakfast for everyone. It was a nice ending to a good visit. Sam said, 'Here we go, Fro, hope you ready.'

Final Regular Season Game

There was one game left for UVA regular football season. I took my youngest daughter and two oldest granddaughters. We would stay with Sam. I was glad it was a home game. Sam told me my cousin, the preacher would be there too. So would some of the mentors. It would be interesting to see Jerome Larkin again. Wonder what smart remarks he would have this time. Too bad for him he would be on my turf now. Sam said without words to be good. It was a sunny cold day. We were all layered. I had on jeans and a $\frac{3}{4}$ fur coat that gathered in the waist. Mimi made the coat. The College President was in a box suite. I didn't want to sit too far away so Cee could hear me yelling for them. It was his senior year and I was proud of him. He would get his degree and maybe go to the Pro's. Sam asked me to come give him a kiss. I told the girls to stay there. I could feel the stares but ignored them. The team was almost finished with warm-ups. Sam hugged me and kissed me with his hand at the top of my hips.

I hit him in his chest, he pretended it hurt. The team ran over and Cee grabbed my arm. I hugged him and all of the others got in line and hugged me as they went to the locker room. If anybody hugged me too long or tight, Coach ushered them on. Sam said they appreciated the prayer at the start of the season. The assistant coaches tried to hug me but Sam said no, hand shake only. He kissed my forehead and high-fived me before he went to the locker room also. He said without words, 'Lots of people want to know why the team loves you and was I wearing real fur.' I laughed.

Prejudged by PETA

As I went to my seat, I had a big smile on my face cause Sam was telling me what some of the people were saying about me. He told me a lady from PETA was waiting near me to ask about the fur. He said not to be mean, the children were here and so were a lot of our friends. He said Jerome was near also.
I had almost made it back to my seat when a lady stood up, announced she was a member of PETA and proceeded to confront me.

She objected to me wearing animal fur because it was inhumane to kill an animal for its fur. She spoke loud enough for everyone in the area to hear her, including my babies. Everyone stopped and looked at her, then me. Some people told her to shut up, sit down and mind her own business. I smiled at her and said, 'woman I have to give it to you cause you have a lot of nerve to show who you really are. But I'm proud of you for standing up for something other than yourself. The definition of prejudice is this. You could have asked me if it's real or fake. By the way, what I wear is none of your damn business and this is the last time I'm explaining it. This is three yards of material from the fabric store that cost forty dollars a yard. It comes in basic colors and a few other odd colors. I would have gotten more but it cost too much to make a full length coat.' I unzipped it to show her the lining which was material with the eternal love symbol on it. I said, 'I'm warm, you're cold. She looked down. I said, 'Here, try it on and tell me the truth.'

She said, 'I'm not putting on your coat.' I said, 'Come on, you started this.' I took the coat off, revealing an orange sweater and jeans and a fine body to fill it. The men said, 'Damn!' She put the coat on. I said, 'So, are you cold?' She said no! I took my phone out and grabbed her and took a selfy photo. She said, 'wait!' It was too late. I told her to give me the coat back; I put it on and zipped it back up. I told her out loud that she better be glad my babies were here and that Coach Max was my boyfriend because on another day and time, I would have tagged her ass. I said out loud, 'Ask before you assume, damn!'

Sam said without words, 'There goes my baby!' I laughed to myself, responding, 'You're stupid!' He said that Jerome heard me and saw me when I took the coat off. He was thinking how lucky he was to get next to this fine woman. Little does he know luck has nothing to do with it. He said my cousin the preacher heard my response and was proud his cousin didn't go old school and assault the lady or cuss her out. A lot of others were thinking they didn't know Coach Max had it like that.

I responded without words to Sam that I won't go off over stupid stuff but will have fun at the last regular season game. I yelled a lot during the game for Cee and the others. It was fun. I even yelled for the coaches. The girls had fun laughing at me. They (UVA) won.

Met Sam's NFL Team

Coach sent out a blast to meet at his house after the game. My cousin and Jerome were coming. There were a few others also. Coach Max gave an interview after the game. The team was awarded ACC Champs and we were going to the Orange Bowl, National Championship game. This was good for Sam. The girls and I stood on the bottom bleachers while Sam gave the interview. When they asked him who or what inspired him. He said the love of a good woman doesn't hurt. He looked at me. I blew him a kiss. Without words Sam asked me to take the girls to da house and get them comfortable because food would be arriving soon. He wanted me at the house to greet his friends.

The food was delivered shortly after we got to da house. It smelled so good. It was baked chicken, jerk chicken breast, ackee and saltfish and fried split shrimp. There were plantains, rice and gravy and coco muffins. I sat down and laughed. The girls asked what I was laughing about. I said it was the look on that woman from PETA's face.

Sam said without words, 'You think I'm playin with you woman? No matter what else I'm doing, I have you on my mind too. We're not on the ship anymore...I told you not to sleep on me. I know you thought and think I've forgotten but I haven't. I know you and you complete me. There's no way I'm treating you any different than when we got to know each other. I love you woman, don't forget it because I won't!' I responded, 'Ok...Jedi Master, Max! I got you!'

He said, 'Start feeding the girls before the guests come.' Jerome was the first to arrive. I should have known he knew where Sam lived and has been here before. He made sure he pulled in close to the house so he would be one of the last to leave.

He offered his hand, I shook it sports style by clutching at the end of our fingers. He asked had I forgiven him yet. I responded that I would know after today. He laughed and said ok! I introduced him to the girls. He smiled hard and told them how pretty they were. Sounded like a neutral line that I could agree with. I asked him to help himself to drinks and the food. He wanted to have a drink and warm up first. My cousin came next. He knew where Sam lived too. He parked behind Jerome so I knew he would stay awhile. I was kind of glad. I didn't feel alone with him there with all these men.

Sam rushed in right behind him and went upstairs to change clothes. I hugged my cousin and introduced him without thinking, to Jerome. He said, 'I already know Mr. Larkin.' I looked at Jerome and said, 'Really?' Jerome shook his head no. My cousin saw the girls and said, 'So these are my younger cousins huh? Come give your cousin a hug.' They came over and told him their names and hugged him. He asked one of them to get him a bottle of water. They did.

He was hungry so I pointed him to the food. I said to Sam without words, 'we will be talking about this mister!!' He didn't answer and I know he heard me. Sam came downstairs with a smile on his face. He grabbed me around my waist and pulled me to him. He kissed me with tongue and then hugged me tight.

He said, 'Thanks baby for all your help. The team sent that but I will thank you my own way later.'

The girls laughed out loud. Sam smiled at them and told them that they must know he loved me. They said, 'Yeah, we know.' One of my granddaughters said they weren't used to seeing anyone kissing me like that. We looked funny. He told them to get use to it because he had no plans of stopping, not even for the 'A team!' That really tickled them. No one called them that but me. All of their names began with an 'A'. My youngest said they were going in the room to watch TV and play games. The doorbell rang, Sam answered. It was a few men I had not seen before. The assistant coaches came in afterwards.

The President, Mr. Blusteen and the Athletic coordinator came in last. It was twelve men there. Sam asked my cousin to pray for us. He did! Everyone said AMEN. The living room was large with more than enough room for all of them. They mingled, talked, ate and drank. When they were seated, they clapped for Sam. I did too! He smiled and thanked everybody for their support and friendship. He agreed that the team did very well this season. They are geeked about the bowl game too. One of the men told Sam he looked different. Sam pointed to me. The guys looked at me. They all smiled. Even the president smiled. Sam said without words that he can't repeat all of what they were thinking about me. They thought I had caught him and blew his mind, little did they know. Sam said only my cousin knew!

Sam said, 'Let me say this to you all so you know exactly where I stand with that woman. They looked at him like reporters at a news conference. Sam said, 'Baby, pull your chair over here.'

I looked at him and shook my head no! It hit me that I had on that same sexy sweater and jeans. Sam said without words 'Too late.' He came over and pulled me up, took my chair and put it next to his then reached for my hand to come with him. He said, 'She's shy around this many men at once, but I'm training her.' They laughed. He said 'The only people that know her better in this house right now, other than her girls are her cousin, Pastor Deon and me. GOD created this woman for me.

Some of you may have thought I was gay because I avoided a lot of women and have rarely been seen with a woman. I was waiting for this woman. I didn't know at first that she was Deon's cousin. (I found out after more than a year later when I showed Deon her photo.) He couldn't believe I was looking for his cousin. Turns out she's a regular woman, so she thinks, and has been hiding from me. Well, she's my woman now and I love everything about her. She's fine as hell; I know all of you see that. She's real and doesn't take a lot of crap from people. She knows where I'm going with football and she's coming with me.

She knows I love her and I know she loves me. She doesn't tolerate being disrespected so if you challenge her, I may not be around to help you. She knows how to fight.' They all laughed. Deon spoke up and said, 'It's true...our cousins taught her...they were boys. But she's a lady and will probably cuss you out if you cross her instead of fighting. As a matter of fact I'm sure she carries a taser.' I laughed out loud! How did you know D? I know you, girl.

Sam said, 'On a serious note...this is my lady and I'm not giving her back ever. She is off limits to any of you, sexually. No matter what anyone says about me, they will be lying if they say I'm with anyone other than this woman.' He squeezed my hand.

He asked me if I had anything to say. I said, 'No! Except I do love Sam and I'm not giving him back either. I'm not with him for money. I do need and want his love. Money can't buy true love anyway. Whenever I'm in your presence, what you do or say will not be repeated by me, so don't ask your wife or partner to ask me cause I'm not telling.

Unless your name is Jerome and then I will sing like a bird.' He laughed and said 'Come on Fro, I said I'm sorry.' Deon asked, 'Sorry about what?' Jerome said he thought Sam brought me as a prearranged date to a recent event that Sam never brought a date to before.

'I hurt her feelings when I told her I would pay her double what Sam paid her to come with him. I hurt her and apologized when I realized she was his girlfriend for real. Fro, please give me another chance, I'm sorry!' I got up and went over to Jerome who stood up. I hugged him and said 'Ok. I forgive you.' Sam introduced the others who were ministers from the local church he attended and a few others from the NFL. They were Sam's friends. Now they were gonna help me too! Sam said without words that's the plan. 'To GOD be the Glory!' I said, 'AMEN!' Sam went on to share that he was looking for another winning season, but would make NFL Coach inquiries the following year. The President said he would back Sam's efforts.

All the men agreed. Sam thanked them and said he will not forget where he came from.

He would help any of them that needs or wants his help, if and when the time comes. He told them he trusted them but will call them on bullshit. He said, 'I'm the same except I'm in love too. I don't have to babysit Fro. She can hold her own when she needs to, besides GOD has called her for a purpose too. She can tell you about it another time.'

The President and Student Activities Coordinator said they had to leave now. Mr. Blusteen asked if he could meet the children. I said, 'Of course.' I went to the door and asked them to come out for a minute. I introduced them to everyone and told them their names and ages. I even mentioned my youngest may be coming to UVA next fall, which means the others would be around also. I told the men I would kill for these babies. They said that won't be necessary, they will also look out for them. I almost cried when I told them thanks.

The President wanted coco muffins. I fixed it by putting a few in a baggie. He wanted jerk chicken too.

When they left the preachers said they had things to do to prepare for tomorrow's service. The team was going to their church with us tomorrow. The guy from the NFL commission said he had a date.

So Jerome and Deon were left. We sat around, laughed and talked for a few more hours. I felt better about Jerome after spending more time with him in Sam's presence. Sam discussed subjects with them that he wouldn't have with the others. He spoke with me without words at the same time. So, he was having two conversations at once. I wanted to learn to do it too. He said without words that I would be able to soon.

The next day we all went to church. The Pastor brought the WORD and everyone enjoyed themselves. The campus bus brought the team and came back to pick them up.

We all had a really good time. The girls and I left to go home after we had dinner with Sam.

Business & Pleasure

He said without words that it would be three or four weeks until the championship game which will be held in Florida. We will be staying at the condo there. He wanted our parents and family to come. He said Nan, Poppy, Michael and Carlo would be there too. We would decide if anyone would stay with us at the condo or all of them would stay at a hotel. For now he wanted me to go to a few Pro games with him. I agreed.

The next weekend he came to Va. Beach for the weekend. We worked on the retirement plan for C&S Mining. The research was completed and the program was ready to be implemented. Sam wanted me to go back to Cozumel in a few weeks to set everything up. He said I would have to be careful because he would only be able to communicate with me by telephone. He laughed. I said, 'Stop playin, boi! You know you can hear me no matter where I am on this earth.' He said, 'You're right, I can and so can you, woman. We are connected for the rest of this life.' I asked if Jacob could do the same.

He said, 'Yes, to everyone but you and I. 'I replied, 'I hope Jacob was not able to hear us making love. He advised that he can't hear our personal conversations. I thought if he could, he would sure want to duplicate it with a woman in his town. I wondered if he had the same over growth as Sam. Sam said no he didn't.

Little Friend, Little Friend

Before he left for Charlottesville, we made sweet love. We rubbed each other down from head to toe. Neither of us attempted a massage. We thought we would leave that to the professionals. We both touched each other every inch of our bodies. It felt good to me. I ran my hands from his head down his face, neck, arms, fingers, chest, stomach, thighs, legs, feet, toes, but and back. He did the same to me. The touches were not hard, but also didn't tickle. It made us want to kiss with the same passion. We did for awhile. I could have sworn my soft spot called my little friend. He seemed to be moving toward her on his own. Sam whispered in my ear that he's ready. I responded I know he is, but are you?

(Direct challenge saying I know and you know I know too!) He bit my ear lightly, this was Sam's choice. He moved me into an easier position so his little friend had easy access. He grew harder and harder. The head went inside my soft spot. I tried to push so he could go deeper but Sam held me in place. **(Giving me a chance to try and run)** He said, 'I know you noticed that my little friend seems to be able to move on his own.

Well, don't be scared baby but, he can. He has chosen you and unfortunately for you he has been allowed to taste her and she tasted him back. He would drive me crazy if I did anything to mess up his position with her. **(What the Hell??? Where's the red light? Wait for it... Froo??... Panic almost set inside me but Sam kept talking...)** She is perfect for him. So it must be true, 'there's someone for everyone. **(random thoughts were filling my head...The flesh is strong...The devil is a liar!... Can we say, 'mutant'!!)** But what's more important is the fact that, my soul loves your soul.'

I moaned in pleasure to the sound of those words, while my flesh felt the same. It was a very peaceful feeling. Not sure yet if we're twin flames or soul mates. There is a difference. I felt totally relaxed and decided to let Sam be himself, without judgment from me. So what, if he was what most people would think is weird. Some folks would be afraid of Sam **(Like I should have been)**. But I wasn't. My head asked, 'Why you not scared? You should be!'

GOD had to be the one that set this up. I am really feeling this dude. I never expected this would happen after so many years of suppressing that voice inside of me. I was preparing to be alone without a mate. As if on cue, when I gave in and took my hands off, GOD took over and changed my plan to His plan. His plan has benefits.

Sam's little friend is now my little friend and my little friend knows exactly how I like it. She too has a mind of her own and loves Sam's little friend. Anything else is a lie. Our little friend rubbed his head side to side inside my soft spot and starting moving further in.

I lifted my hips to meet him. The adventure was breathtaking. We all enjoyed it more than words can say. **(That is crazy to say out loud)** Sam left for home and a work week. He was not only the players Coach; he was the assistant coaches Coach too. He had a style that was unique also. The players liked the style because it allowed them to play smarter not harder. If the opponent was very large in size they needed to be physical to get the point understood that they would bring it even if they had to do it in TWOS! Sam said without words that there are many ways to win. His advantage was almost unfair when you really think about it. He said, 'Your prayer was the only reason they won. They were not only physically healthy, they were mentally healthy too.' This was a real Halleluiah moment.

The Business Plan

Sandy called and said Carlo wanted twenty five percent of her business if he gave her all the money up front. She said she didn't want to have a partner, right now.

I told her I would consider funding her with
no business repayment plan if she presented a
business plan that she was willing to stand
behind if given the opportunity.

She said, 'So Fro what do I have to do for this
possible, opportunity? Have you and Sam's
baby?' I was a little stunned because I didn't
think she actually took me serious. Got to give
it to Sandy, she paid a lot of attention. I
know she would love to have Sam's baby.

Sam said without words, I told you to leave
that alone but you won't. She doesn't want to
have my baby as much as she wants to carry
your baby. She loves you Fro! You have the
confidence she wishes she had. The love you
have in our relationship is desired by many.

I responded that I know and am sure that to
whom much is given, much is required. And
please don't think I forgot that you
introduced me to her and your Godmothers
hair potion. You knew who she was and wanted
a way to let her be the initial distributor for
Nan's hair potion. You know Nan would give
her that stuff if we had a baby and let her
keep the child for any length of time.

Don't play me Sam! He laughed and tried to say it wasn't true but I knew it was. I told Sandy Sam and I would have to be in a committed relationship for me to really consider that. She said she knew we were committed to each other no matter what I said. (She was really challenging my excuse) I responded, 'Okay. Sandy your pay back will be to carry me and Sam's baby when it's time. Will you do that?' She said yes before the words could leave my space good. She drove two and a half hours to bring me her proposal the next day. Chick was ready. I talked it over with Sam. He was in agreement. I gave Sandy the money she needed for her business. She told me she would be up and running when I moved there. She wanted me to let her care for me and my girl's hair. I had to speak with Nan about the hair potion. I wanted to know about it too. I would speak with her when she came to the game.

JACOB
Sam said without words that Jacob is going to call me.

I was excited because I wanted to speak with him, too. After we verbally loved on each other, he told me he wanted a business plan too. I told him I would call him back when I was better prepared to write down what he wants. I will bring it so he can sign it. (This was a setup to go back to Jamaica.) He agreed and made me promise I would wear his last two designs. Sam said without words I better be careful making promises to Jacob. He might create something I may not want to wear.

I replied that I would wear it anyway even if it's only once. It is more about his work being seen and liked, than money. 'I'm proud of him, Sam.' He responded he was proud of me for embracing Jacob so wholeheartedly. He told me Jacob loves me. Jacob is a whole story of his own. Even from the start. Imagine the raw, enhanced, got another sense to kick in and lost his sense of sight later, person who lived. He was scared as a child. Always having to hide when he was always, 'IT.' But GOD covered and kept him and used Sam to the degree he has been used this far.

Jacob could be walking in divine providence. He obviously has more human qualities than his reptile side. But that reptile side is deep. He has to be an excellent swimmer. The predatory nature of a reptile is my biggest concern. Sam was going to explain this to me because I know he knows.

Maybe he's been waiting for a good time to tell me. I knew Sam and Jacob heard me. Nan probably heard me too.

Before any unspoken or verbal words were spoken, I jumped in and said, 'Lord, I'm here for you! Because I'm here, I know you are here also. I'm not afraid because I have forty years of good health given to me by You, Lord. Imagine if the love I can pour into Jacob has healing properties. I wonder if Jacob can be healed, through me, by GOD. Of course, he can! This is the answer Jacob is waiting for me to give him.'

Without words I said, 'Sam either this has been your motive all along, you know how I felt that you want something other than sex or you are blessed by GOD himself for looking after this wounded child named Jacob.'

Sam said, 'The latter, baby! So now you know how I feel too. This is all so overwhelming to me too. I thank GOD everyday for sending you my way. This would be too hard alone and much harder without you. Thus my argument of, I'm not letting you out of my life. The sex is off the chain and I'm whipped now but so are you. You promised me already, Fro! Besides I have forty years to pester you if you want to play Love and War!' He laughed. I laughed too! It wasn't long ago that I had those exact thoughts about Sam.

Professional Football Game

The week had gone by fast. It was Friday and we were going to a Pro game on Sunday. Sam would come pick me up in his plane at Newport News airport, on Saturday. We would be going to the game in Jacksonville, Fl. Sam said it was too far to drive, in a short time. The Jaguars would be playing Dallas. There would be will call tickets from the owner for Sam and I. He wanted to talk to Sam about plays and the team. When we arrived, Sam gave instructions to be prepped to go back Sunday night, by midnight. A car with driver was waiting for us. We were taken to an area near the stadium. He said he rented a condo for two days. The condo was nice. It was in a high rise building near the stadium. Literally, we could see it from the window. Sam said dinner is being held at the owner's house. I was wondering about all of this. It seemed like a lot. I was beginning to feel out of place like this was someone else's life. The college I could relate to but this was something else. These are wealthy people and I'm not.

I sure don't want to make Sam look bad in their presence. All I could think about was I'm not ready and Sam deserves a more seasoned woman for this. I went in the bedroom to find my bag. I needed to smoke a joint. Sam came in before I could get to my bag. He pulled me to him and hugged me. He said it was okay to feel overwhelmed, but remember that I am a millionaire also. But more than that we have been blessed with gifts from GOD! No weapon formed... we hugged hard and kissed passionately. Sam assured me that he would be with me. He would not leave me with any of them until I was more comfortable. He told me to remember Cozumel, the beach party and the coach's ball. Hold his hand if I was nervous or uncomfortable. I agreed but still smoked half the joint. I took a shower, dressed in a short mini blue skirt with a peach cardigan sweater. My three inch pumps worked well also. Sam said I was too sexy for them so I had to stay near him, so he could feel my breast on the low. I laughed hard. Sam said he was hungry and so was I.

We walked down to the condo lobby. A car was waiting. It took fifteen minutes to get to the owner's home.

Sam asked if I was ready, I said I was hungry and could we ask for a snack if dinner wasn't ready. We weren't inside but a few minutes when dinner was served. It almost seemed like they were waiting for us. Mr. Whitsel, JAX Jaguars owner seems to be laid back. His wife acted like she was ADHD. She was talking and moving fast. We ate in the dining room. There are only five couples here and Sam and I are the only people of any other color here but I didn't care. The food smelled good.

Mr. Whitsel asked Sam was he nervous about the Championship game in a few weeks.

Sam told him, yes of course, this is uncharted territory for him but he was up for the task. Sam said without words, 'Here we go Fro. Be good woman.' Mr. Whitsel asked us to call him David. He asked me how I was adjusting to life under a microscope. I told him my life isn't under a microscope yet.

He said, 'Come on Fro, I saw the YouTube video from your cruise with Sam. I'm also aware the PETA lady tried to provoke you at the last game. How are you so cool with that? Lots of people want to now and will want to know who caught this eligible man.'
I laughed and responded, 'I'll refer them to the video! I have a teenage daughter who I will protect at all cost. There will be a warning shot over the bow if I feel like my kid is being threatened.' David laughed so hard, he almost spit out his food. I told him that on a serious note, until Sam and I decide we want to be married to each other, I don't feel obligated to open up my private life, unless I want to. People can take all the shots they want at Sam or me for that matter. But when it comes to my baby and my grandbabies, I don't play no shit. I will find out how to make sure they never mention my babies again. David said, 'well don't ever worry about me because I'd never cross that line.' Sam said without words, 'he means it Fro.' I replied to David that I appreciated his understanding regarding the crossing of that line.

I told him that my hands were full with checking the women before me, about Sam. I told him one woman called me a bitch because Sam wouldn't date her. I had to make Sam talk to her and tell her where he stood with her. Ms. Whitsel asked me how it worked out. I told her let's just say she will think twice or more before she confronts me again. She wanted to know more I told her we could talk later. She agreed.

Sam said without words that she's being bullied and needs to speak up for herself but she's had problems with self esteem. She knows having ADHD must look like she's a burden but she's not. She hardly ever ask Mr. Whitsel for anything. He gives her an amount every year that she spends any way she wants. She loves him but he doesn't defend her in front of others. This hurts her. David said he doesn't get involved with that. I asked how he could allow others to disrespect his wife and say nothing. He said his wife was strong.

I said, 'Then she's stronger than me and I
have to know how she does it because if Sam
allowed his old or new flame to disrespect me
and do nothing, he'd be breaking up a fight,
cause I would hit the bitch.' David laughed
out loud, so did his wife. Sam spoke up and
told us that he loves me and would never allow
another woman to challenge me, over him. No
other woman can win because I'm not giving
you back baby, ever!

I said, 'Awww' and kissed him. David continued
and asked, 'when are you two getting married?'
Sam answered saying we've only been dating
five months. We need a little more time to
know for sure because neither of us will ever
do this again. David responded that was good.
We moved on to other subjects. I felt more
comfortable after dinner. Sam said without
words he wanted to speak with the guys about
business. He wanted to know if I was okay
with the ladies. I responded yes. Sam asked
David if they could discuss a few things in the
study. David was more than ready. The ladies
stayed in the dining room and chit chatted.

I asked them if they believed in GOD! They all said yes. I asked them if it's okay if we pray for the woman of this house because our sister needs to be lifted. Ms. Whitsel put her hand to her mouth and a tear fell. I hugged her and told her it was okay, GOD loves her. We all held hands and I prayed for her and the others.

I asked that she be healed and be given courage to continue this race. I asked GOD to send a comforter so she never feels alone again.

We all said AMEN then helped her clear the table. She complimented me on my hair and outfit. She asked me if I had a breast job. I told her no. She commented that she's sure Sam likes them. I said No! He loves them and they love him too. Everybody laughed!

Sam said without words he was tired and ready to go. He asked me to come over and love on him. I did! Sam said David and another guy wondered what I looked like without clothes. Too bad they will never know. I sat in his lap. He covered my chest with his arm and rubbed my thigh.

This made the men uncomfortable but no one moved, they just looked and smiled. Sam said, 'My woman, and laughed! He told them he really loved me and was glad GOD sent me his way. He said, 'I don't share!' I kissed his lips and got lost for a moment. I stopped suddenly and apologized. I said, 'I forgot where I was for a moment.' Sam said, 'That's okay!' We should go. We thanked David for dinner and said we'd see him tomorrow at the game. I hugged the ladies and we left.
Sam said, 'they like you baby.' They think we are a nice, sexy couple.

We're Getting Married

On the ride back to the condo, Sam asked me again when was I moving to Charlottesville with him. I told him when my baby graduated from high school and after our family vacation. He asked if we can get married in the islands with our family there. I knew he wanted me to have my dress made soon. He said yes he did. I told him, yes! He stopped and turned to me with a big smile. 'You'll marry me?" I repeated yes.

He held me and kissed me so softly but with power. I almost lost my breath.

When we got back to the condo, he snatched me up as soon as we got in the door. He picked me up, pushed my skirt up and began to feel me up. He pulled up my sweater, found my breast and sucked them with such passion, I moaned loudly. I was so wet; he laid me on the couch and sucked down all my juices. It felt so good cause I was more comfortable that this was my man who wanted me and my body. We were making rough and tumble love tonight. We slept in each other's arms.

Sam was happy at the game the next day. He told the owner who congratulated us.

He only left me once the whole day and that's when he went to meet the Jaguar Coach. His hands were on me the rest of the day. It felt good. All I could think was, don't let me find out this really my dude that I can and will vibe with and enjoy the rest of my life. How many people really can say they have experienced that?

Wouldn't it be wonderful to know, if most people experienced that as opposed to, only a few people knowing how it feels to VIBE with a mate that GOD actually sent to you.

Wow! Sam said without words, 'Now you are getting it. You know, what I've been trying to say to you woman since we met. I'm really not giving you back to anyone else except me...I promise to love you every day! You are the woman created by GOD for me...you know that rib, the missing bone...I'm glad you are having the opportunity to experience this lifestyle and all of me. We are happy and having fun while being in position when GOD assigns a task and we comply. No! Happily comply with His Request!

Someone once said, 'Everybody want to be famous but somebody has to do the work!' Well Fro, we doing da work while trying not to be famous and well known.

There are many that are affected by what we do and don't do. The 'A-team' for example, together and healthy they would be fierce and grow to handle some shit and give as much as they get. Infamous Nan is a story of her own.

Jacob is a story of his own. Michael and Carlo are stories of their own. Not to mention Mimi and Sandy. A lot of people's lives are tied to ours. Good and Bad!' I responded, 'Us being in position allows others to be in their position to be blessed on earth by GOD.

Okay...You said all of that and I said yes! I'll marry you. What would you have to say if I had said no? Wait...I do not want to hear your answer to that question...it'll be too long. I laughed... hard... Sam finally laughed too.

'Fro, we gonna have so much fun at the college next year. I'm finally gonna have the fun I've always wanted while working and living at the college.' I answered, 'Yeah but you got me on the fast track plan. You have me skipping grades to Pro with little experience and expecting for me to blend in with ease. Although I have to admit we do vibe very well and this without words ability does help.

You do make business fun, while allowing me to be myself and love on you at the same time. We are equally matched sexually and Lord knows it's good. No! Very Good!'

Sam said, 'So...you just want my body and my mind to keep sexing you while you feel more comfortable when you skip grades to the Pros?' I responded yes without looking at Sam. I smiled; he pushed me over and caught my shoulder with his other arm. We had that entire conversation and no one knew but us! Boy this was really fun. I can hardly wait for it. This last year of practice, learning about people and how to redirect them when they are wrong and you know it.

I was thinking it would be so nice for others to experience Tortuga Rum and accessories, the unique jewelry of Jamaica, the Blue Tortoise cream and hair tonic from the Caymans, 3Seats by way of the silver and die cast of Cozumel. Sam responded, 'You would have to have the buy in of the others because they are the ones that will be affected the most. Some things may have to stay a mystery. He explained that 3Seats may have to compensate for other things. Ultimately this is about the glory of GOD, anyway. I said, 'baby you alright with me.' Dallas beat JAX.

The owner told Sam, he would not forget him or me. We left the game and prepped to go home. We would leave at 6 am so I could drive home in the morning time after rush hour traffic. Love tonight is priceless. After showers and rub downs we were ready for some deep love. I have agreed to marry this man. I'd always said I would never marry again after my husband died.

I never expected to meet him, but I have met him and his name is Samuel. I've tried to not love him. I can't deny who Sam is in my life and besides there's no one that completes me more than him. He wanted control and I complied. The love was so sweet I almost cried.

We were taking off at 6:30 am - the weather was beautiful. We became members of the 40k ft mile high club. I have to say it was fun. I got home before my youngest got home from school.

Nan's Plan

The rest of the week was spent looking for a location to house products and make sure they are secure.

Once the 3Seats piece was created, I will store them nearby for distribution. I'll also store the hair tonic if Nan approves. Since it will be two weeks before I see Nan, I called her to see what the possibilities were. She started out asking if I had any complications from the hair tonic or the tortoise items. I told her no. She asked if the conch oil was working. I responded yes and thank you for it. I couldn't help but jump right in. 'Nan, do you have a supply of the hair tonic?' She said, 'I have quite a bit already made and I only make more when I'm almost out.'

I asked how she stored it. She said in a dark, cool place. Plastic bottles were good but glass worked better, no metal. She said, 'So, you want to sell it but want to know if you can get a supply?' I responded that I am helping Sam's friend who did my hair on the ship. She's opening a hair salon of her own.

Lots of women could use help due to aging and medication, like cancer medicine. It will not be sold to just anyone. That would cause too many questions. I was going to help my immediate family with what I already have. She told me the shampoo I have now is just for me. The conditioner can be used by anyone. Curiosity got the better of me. I asked her how she could create that shampoo for me without meeting me first?

She was silent for a moment and began a short tale that left me speechless. She said she's known about me for a long time. She felt my spirit when I cruised to the islands years ago. She knew then that it was only a matter of time before Sam found me. I was created by GOD for Sam and this hour. The Holy Spirit told her what would make my hair conform and look beautiful at the same time. The red is the color of blood and represents the fact that I will be in Jesus' presence one day. But as for now, He knows me. Tears were running down my face and my heart was so glad to be loved by GOD. At that moment, I couldn't speak. Nan said, 'Come on Fro don't stop now.'

I asked Nan if she would send some hair tonic for my family and friends. She said, 'Yes, I will ship it tomorrow.' I asked if I could get a supply for Sandy's salon. She said, 'Yes, you can. I will send a supply four times a year.' 'Nan, can you show me how to make it?' She said when I come back for a visit, she'll show me. I was so excited by this! I told Nan it would be next year before we approached Sandy about a baby. Nan said, 'You mean babies? Your egg and Sam's sperm may produce two or three babies. I can hardly wait.' I said, 'So Nan, you knew this was going to happen? Did Sam know also?'

She said, 'Sam is the only one to answer that. I was the one who noticed Sammy was special and told his mom, Kalisa. When his mom got sick I tried to help but Kalisa was sick for too long before she asked for help. She loved that boy and protected him because she knew GOD was gonna use him for good. He was too young to go to the US with his father, who didn't know how to care for such a small child, so Kalisa asked me to care for him.

I spent a lot of time in Jamaica while Kalisa tried to get well and so Sammy could still help Jacob. I discovered that Jacob and Sammy were special. He would not leave Jacob so I gave Sam money to help Jacob so he would come with me to the Cayman's. I was ready to go home after Kalisa died. She would have loved you Fro. You and Sam's child or children may possess favor from GOD. I would recognize it and help them deal with the knowledge. That is why Nan and Poppy still holding on. We have a mission from GOD also.' She said, 'Fro welcome to my family and we love you!' I responded thanks and I love them too! We hung up the phone. I was still stunned. Sam said without words that he was glad I finally knew. I asked him if he could speak with Nan like he does me. He said no. He said he and I are the only ones with that luxury. He said Nan can't read his mind but he can read hers and he's never told her. He said Nan can sense me but can't fully read mine either. He said it must be how GOD wants it. Who are we to say different?

Retirement Plan in Cozumel

I told Sam we needed a ride to Cozumel next weekend. I wanted to take my youngest and granddaughters, the 'A-Team.' He said that would be great. I needed to setup the retirement plan on their computer and check on the diecast.

Carlo picked us up. He liked the girls; they spoke very little at first, and then let loose at the house. Carlo hadn't had that much noise in the house in a long time. He smiled a lot when the youngest started asking him questions. He was put on the spot. I laughed a lot. The girls and I settled in Sam's quarters. He had a king size bed so all of us could sleep together.

Mimi came over and cooked for us.

Carlo asked me to go to a party with him tonight. Mimi said she'd stay with the girls. I wore my halter dress from last summer. It was 75 degrees at night in December. We rode in the Hummer for about fifteen minutes before coming to a neighborhood with stores downstairs. We parked and went into a storefront. The music was fast and spicy. We sat at the bar.

I got a text on the phone from Sam. He said it appears there is some interference.
He can't hear me. He told me to be careful. No sooner then I responded okay, a lady comes in and straight up to Carlo. She points at me and snaps her fingers. I sit straight up just in case I have to defend myself. I don't say anything because this is not about me. I heard Carlo say Sam's name. The lady looks at me, smiles and walks away.
Carlo asked me if I knew how to dance salsa. I said no but I could learn. He pulled me up and led me to the dance floor. He got behind me and held my hips on each side. He guided my hips from left to right. Twisting like the number eight. We did this for about five minutes. I was getting aroused having the sides of my behind rubbed like that. I know I felt a semi hard penis too. Carlo was friendlier towards me this trip. I wondered was it due to the girls or 3Seats. I sat back down. Carlo left me to go dance with the woman that appeared to have fussed at him. They salsa danced great. I was on my second Dos Equis, but Carlo was drinking Tequila.

Respect the Conch

I watched him take three shots. I knew I would be driving home. The bartender spoke English. I asked him to draw a map of how I get back to Carlo's house. He did.

As I sat back, a nice man asked me to dance. We danced salsa and then a soulful song came on. We danced slow but apart. He two stepped. Carlo watched us with a smile. When I came back to my seat, he was ready to go. We left. I asked Carlo to let me drive at least ten minutes. He helped me in the driver's seat putting his hands on my behind to push me in. He got in on the other side, stumbling a bit. As the road got darker, Carlo put his head on my shoulder and cupped one of my breasts. He told me how good it felt. I pushed his hand away. We made it to the house. Mimi was on the couch asleep. I woke her to thank her. She said she was leaving. I checked on the girls. They were asleep all over the bed. I figured I'd take a quick shower and sleep on the couch.

I put on a t-shirt and went downstairs to get a drink and a spot on the couch. Carlo came downstairs and caught me in the kitchen. He started dancing behind me and felt my hips and breast. I moved away quickly knowing he was very intoxicated. I told Carlo the girls were all over the bed so I was sleeping downstairs. He said I could sleep in his room he won't bother me. **(Why would I believe an intoxicated man?)** He knew I loved Sam so I assumed it would be okay. I followed him upstairs! **(Totally wrong answer)** He had a king bed also. I laid on the edge, too tired and sleepy to recognize the trap. A trap I unknowingly helped to set. Carlo turned off the light. I was almost asleep when I realized he was close behind me and started rubbing my behind and thighs. He reached over me, cupped my breast and squeezed. He quickly repositioned me and started sucking my breast. I automatically started getting wet. I tried to get up but I was weak from the beer and being sleepy, I had been up a long time. He gripped my thighs, tasted my soft spot and moaned when he tasted my juices.

I was embarrassed to be in this position. When Carlo tried to penetrate me, I told him Sam would hurt him and he knew it was true. He said he didn't know why he was so horny though. He asked me to let him masturbate, while he proceeded to do just that. He didn't wait for my response. He sucked my breast, licked my nipples and rubbed between my legs until he came. I got up immediately, went to the bathroom and wiped all juices off. I went ahead and got on the edge of the bed with the kids.

I was almost asleep when I remembered I used the conch oil. This situation was not all Carlo's fault. I would try to never think of it anymore. Glad Sam couldn't hear that. Or maybe he should have.

The girls got up before me. Carlo fixed them breakfast. When I came down, he acted like nothing happened. I was good with that. I was quick to say, 'You had to meet the A-Team before you cooked huh? He had refused to cook for me. He told me to be quiet woman. The girls smiled.

I asked Carlo to take us to the company this morning. I wanted to put the information on the company computer so it would be ready when it was time.

One of the girls entered all the employee's names into the RSC (retirement system computer). At the end of this year, everyone would get $2k. There are 150 employees which equals $300k that should go to the RSC when profits are shared. It was already established that $300k would be distributed to the RSC so even if profits were more, the RSC would only receive the starting $2k per person. The following year profits would be divided into fourths. There were rules; you had to leave all funds for the first year without touching it. Withdrawal request had to be made thirty days ahead of time. The money was stored in the Caymans and had to be picked up, so time was needed for that. The balance could not go below $1k and still work for C&S Mining. I was hoping one day, one of my children could come to Cozumel and help Carlo with office work. After we were done, I asked Carlo for an update on 3Seats.

He took us to his office and then to a locked back room. He made a piece and was working on two others in different sizes. I was impressed with the new mold.

 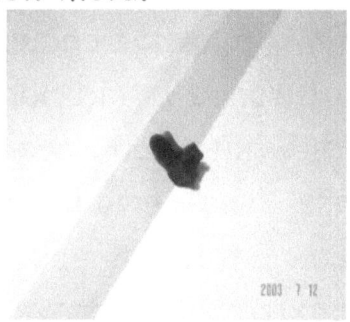

Carlo knew he could craft very well and knew it was his calling. He still wasn't completely ready so I told him to call me when he is and I will come back to check. He said he would bring me a sample when he came to the game. I agreed! The girls wanted to go in the mine itself. They had never been in a mine.
I wanted to also. Carlo took us after we put on hard hats. The tour was fascinating.

I asked Carlo to let me take his truck and he catch a ride home. The girls needed to leave. He said sure. He'd be home later. This gave us time to use the pool.

All of a sudden Sam is speaking to me without words. He told me to be careful this is Mexico. I was glad to speak with him. The girls were in the pool now. I was watching them from a lounge chair.

Without words I told Sam I made an error. He said, 'what? You wore it?' Yes was my response. 'Did Carlo have sex with you?' 'No, he tried. I told him you would hurt him. He was intoxicated. I drove us home from a party he invited me to. He wanted to dance salsa, but felt me up without penetration. He said, 'Fro, I told you to be careful with that stuff! It's potent.' I responded I was kind of sore and thought I could use it while away with the girls. I forgot all about Carlo. I was excited that he wasn't being mean to me. Thought it was due to 3Seats or the girls. Well, at least we both know he's not gay, but he knows how my body feels.

Sam said, 'Not quite. He was kind of drunk and doesn't really remember. He is too afraid to ask you so he will keep it for awhile.' 'Shouldn't I tell him that nothing happened?'

(Sam wants to teach Carlo he's the pack leader of me!) Sam said, 'No, he's trying not to think about your fine body right now. Let him soak.' 'Sam, don't be mean, this is your boi,' I said. He responded, 'right! But you are almost my wife. No one can please you more than me.'

I responded, 'You are absolutely correct. I will respect the oil from here out. This is the first time I've felt free enough to tell the truth when I made a mistake and you issue a firm warning that this life is real. I thank GOD it was Carlo and not someone I have no clue about. I accept the warning and forgiveness now, especially when we are about to get married. I know I'm going to have to tell some fine ass men that I am off the market and our love is going to stand the test of this time. I'm Sam's soon to be wife, can't share Fro!' Sam laughed a lot. He said, 'You crazy woman!' I said, 'And you're out of your mind!' He laughed harder.

The girls were hungry and I was too. They put on swim covers and we went to that taco stand across the street from Mimi's store.

That's the only place I felt safe with the girls and me driving. Sam said, 'I'm with you baby!' The girls loved the tacos. We ate there and they ate a few more native tacos. I took them over to Mimi's shop. They looked around and all saw something they wanted. Mimi smiled at the girls the whole time. I paid her and we went back to the house. The girls got back in the pool. This time I got in too. We played around for about an hour before getting out. Everybody washed their hair. I let them use the conditioner and shampoo Nan sent. They felt their hair change and saw the slight growth. They were excited. I was too. Their hair was soft and beautiful but not straight. Everyone rinsed the conditioner out in the rain forest shower. It was fun!

Sam was at another Pro game for the weekend. But he had time to keep track of me. It was kind of nice knowing this.

Carlo took us sightseeing when he came home. It was a nice afternoon. We left for the airport. I spoke with Carlo outside the hanger explaining he was drunk and even though he felt me up, we didn't have sex.

He seemed relieved. I told him I used Nan's conch oil without thinking about the effects on him. He was good. We left for home. We took my granddaughters home and my youngest and I went home. They were excited about going to Florida for the game.
They loved staying in hotels, especially with a lot of family.
Sam visited me once before he would be in lock down mode to prepare the team for the championship game.
So now I have a Caribbean connection. One of the benefits is the ability to get away, relax and keep fun in my life, only now, I have an exit strategy. I know I'll see Heaven one day, and be welcomed home like the child of GOD that I am. Without words Sam said, 'Amen, Amen and Amen.'

National College Football Championship

The week went by fast. Lots of plans were made. Most of my immediate family came. Sam's dad came. Michael, Carlo, Sandy, Nan and Poppy were here.

It was decided that Nan and Poppy would stay at the hotel with Sam's dad and my mom. So no one stayed at the condo but Sam and I. Everybody flew in. Sam sent the plane to the Caribbean to pick up his peoples. My cousin the Pastor and his immediate family stayed at the hotel with my other relatives. They all took up a whole floor. It was kind of fun. The children really had fun. Their parents were happy to be able to have others looking out for them besides themselves. The hotel was four star with lots for the children to do downstairs near the lobby. We rented a bus to take everyone to the stadium and drop them at the gate. They had their tickets already. We all sat in the same area. The weather was beautiful. The mentors and a few people from the church in Charlottesville are here also. I drove to the game early, while the team practiced.

Sam had me come down for a kiss and hug.
The team hugged me too. I loved those kids.
We yelled a lot and had lots of fun. Finally,
UVA won ACC Championship (Orange Bowl).
We were all so happy for Sam and the team.
Late dining was setup at one of the hotel's
Salons. We hosted our family and friends for
a late dinner at no cost to them. There was
live entertainment throughout the evening.
Karaoke was setup first with the young people
in mind then jazz for the mature people. Sam
invited the football team and their families
too. The college President and his family came
also. We all had a good time talking, laughing
and watching the children. The mature people
seemed to hit it off. Michael was trying to hit
on one of my cousins. It was funny to watch
because his island accent was so thick he had
to keep repeating himself. Carlo and Sandy
talked and laughed too.
Sam and I spoke without words. We were
happy to see almost all the people we love and
know having fun together. We moved around
talking to everyone. I stayed close to Sam as
I had before.

When we finally got back to the condo we got in the hot tub to sooth our aching bodies. That night we made love to both of our satisfaction. It was so intense that I had a few shakes the next day. Everyone went home the next day except me and the Caribbean crew. We all stayed at Sam's condo until Monday.

Carlo brought the sample of 3Seats for my review. I was very impressed. There was one in 3 different sizes. He said the diecast for each size would contain one hundred each. He would have everything completed in another month. It would take that much time to have enough silver on hand and workers to process, monitor the oven and cooling process, buff, attach clasp, insert stones received by Michael in the crease of each seat, (S&M would be selling to me directly a batch of white, black and red diamonds in three sizes for each seat) quality control, boxing and safely storing until it was time for me to pick them up. I reached over and kissed his cheek.

I was so full I shouted all over the room for the wonderful assignment GOD had setup and was about to complete. Carlo was startled and got Nan to come see about me. She came in the room and both of us were shouting. Carlo left the room and closed the door. Poppy and Michael heard us but didn't stop what they were doing or get up.

Commitment with Benefits

Well college football was done for the season. Sam and I attended an NFL playoff game but watched the Super bowl at home. Turns out Cee graduated from college and was drafted by JAX Jaguars, so more celebration was in order.

My youngest graduated from high school in the summer and was accepted as a freshman at UVA in the fall. The college President gave her a full ride scholarship. We were happy for the gesture. Sam and I paid for five more students to go to UVA for free.

Within a month, Mimi had finished my wedding dress. It was so beautiful. We invited and paid for her and her family to come to our wedding.

Sam and I set a date to be married this July in Jamaica. We had dated for a year.

All our family and friends were there by way of cruise ship. GOD allowed a great day. A well known Virginia photographer took the wedding images. Everyone had a great time. Sam's dad was a little upset with thoughts of Sam's mom.

He knew she would be so happy and proud of her son and he was thankful that GOD chose him to be Sam's father. Even Jacob was there in the shadows. The reception was off the chain. Tamia sang at the wedding and performed a short set at the reception. Santana and Kem were awesome. We ended on a Reggae flavor.

Our guests received a bag of keepsakes. The children received native items and items for their age. The teenagers and young adults got iPad minis and jewelry. The mature adults received cigars, joints and island sweets. They all received Maui Jim shades. Nan and Poppy made sure the bags had rum and cake samples included.

Sam and I stayed at our house on our wedding night. GOD came to us in prayer and told us HE loves us and we are Righteous before Him. Another Halleluiah moment!

That night we made love like it was our last day alive. We touched every inch of each other. Our minds included.

By now we knew we had to be twin flames.

A **Twin Flame** is a spiritual concept describing the highest possible form of unconditional love between two souls. Both souls are extremely attracted to each other on every level and are destined to be together. There is a higher purpose for their union. The souls also have a great desire to satisfy and enjoy each other sexually. Telepathic communication happens often. Each twin can pick up on the other's thoughts.

The next day was even more fun. We all partied at the beach. I cried a lot to see so many people display so much love to us and each other. I was so proud to be loved by GOD. Our families, by blood or love are the benefits of committing your life to GOD! We all were seeing this firsthand.

Sam invited the employee's of S&M to the party. He introduced me as his wife. They were happy. Even Monie gave us a hoot hoot! She hugged me and Sam. We told her we loved her, too.

Everyone stayed in Jamaica the whole week and had a real vacation. We all actually spent time with the natives of this city in Jamaica. New friendships were established. Hopefully forever.

Jacob even allowed a few people meet him.
They only saw him from the waist up.
Listening to all those extra thoughts gave him
great joy.
I believe Michael had the most fun. There
were lots of extra single women.
When we got back to VA, it was time for my
youngest to move to Charlottesville, me too.
She moved into the dorm and I moved to the
house. A special family with two children
moved into my house, rent free for two years.
This gave them time to save money to become
debt free. This was their prayer to GOD!
Sam and I were happy to finally be together
more often.
The new football season started. We went to
the MLUC ball as a couple that was moving and
shaking on the line. I decided to wear Jacob's
second design. The weather was cool enough.
I wore the knit/fur outfit. It was a hit. A lot
of ladies asked where to find it. I advised
that it would be available soon. Jacob the
designer wasn't ready to reveal yet.

We visited a few more team owners and had a few dinners at our house near campus. They are all made to feel comfortable, as if this was their home. The owner's were comfortable listening when Sam explained his style and choice of coaching methods.

Sam knew a few owners would be speaking with their current head coaches for confirmation.

My other children took advantage and moved to Jamaica and Cozumel to help with the business of S&M and C&S.

Sam's dad and my mom started hanging out together more often. They said they were just good friends but we thought differently. We didn't question them cause they were grown and our parents. We didn't want to know. They spent a month in the Cayman's with Nan and Poppy. Nan hooked up my mom's hair. Sandy's shop was doing very well.

My youngest and I went to her for our hair care, every week.

3Seats was finally completed in diecast and in three sizes. The cost was $200k for the diecast and storage covers. It was another eight hundred thousand dollars to produce 60k total pieces in three sizes.

The seat comes in small, medium and large. This is to accommodate those who also wear a cross. Incurable illnesses were everywhere. A lot of people needed and wanted 3Seats as an encouraging reminder that they had more options than they realized. It is a reminder that we can talk to GOD anytime we want and He will be there to hear and help us.

In other words, we have to pray! The cross is a reminder that Jesus set us free to be able to know and learn our GOD! Jesus didn't stay on the cross or in the grave.

3 SEATS
are for the Believers
WHO BELIEVE
Jesus is the Son of the living GOD
(Matthew 16,16)
Jesus arose from the dead on the 3rd day
(Luke 24)
ascended into Heaven and now
Christ Jesus now sits on the right hand of GOD
(Mark 16,19)
No one can come to GOD the Father
except through Christ Jesus
(Matthew 11, 25-27)
Who has the power to petition GOD
on our behalf,
(John 6, 31-58)
You, being a joint heir,
(Romans 8, 11-18)
have the right to sit next to Christ Jesus,
Ask whatever you will and it shall be done.
(Ephesians 2, 5-7)

The Question is...
Have You Grown Beyond The Cross?

Sincerely,
Frozine Slater-Morrow

He currently intercedes for us every day. The message was finally getting through that GOD is not dead and does care. He came and sent so that we might have life. 3Seats was sold everywhere I went.

There were invitations to a few women and men conferences. I was almost as busy as Sam but we always found time to touch and spoke without words regularly.

Expanding our Family

Before the end of the next football season, Sandy was ready to carry our baby(s). She had enough regular customers to keep her business running without new clients. Four of my eggs and Sam's sperm was taken and allowed to join and create embryos. This many was implanted because we were not sure if any of them were viable. Sandy had never had children before. All were implanted into Sandy. Three survived and grew. I prayed for her, the babies and went to almost all of her doctor appointments. We read to her and the babies every week. They ate well.

Sam and I spent a lot more time with Sandy so we could be close to the babies. We took turns spending the night with her when she was further along. Her belly was so big it prevented her from some activities. We told her not to worry about gaining weight. The babies would eat it up but we would help her after they were born. When Sam or I rubbed her stomach to quiet the babies and her feet to help with swelling, I imagined it was me. She went 8 months before they were born, two boys and one girl. They were healthy, seven pounds each and so beautiful. Sam and I still had more than thirty five years of good health, so we would see them grow up. Sam was so proud, he cried like a baby so did Sandy. We thanked her for carrying our sweet pumpkins. She said, 'That's it, I'm paid in full!' We laughed and loved on her.

This was the first time he was allowed to love and care for his own children without feeling like he did something wrong and they would be taken away.

That same year Sam was hired by the NFL as Head Coach of the Carolina Panthers. We settled in Charlotte, NC. It wasn't long after Sam met with the team that he asked me to pray for them. I prayed a similar prayer that was shared with the UVA team. The Panthers were healthy and enjoyed playing for Sam. They seemed to welcome his new style and worked hard to go to the Super Bowl.

The babies were pretty popular especially when they were toddlers and out with Sam alone. The baby girl stayed close to dad but talked a lot of baby talk. The boys were always trying to run and spoke very little, in public. After they turned two and a half years old, we allowed them to go stay with Nan and Poppy for awhile. They all fell in love. Nan and Poppy enjoyed finishing their potty training and the terrible twos. It gave them both a reason to get up and live. They poured so much love into those babies.

My mom and Sam's dad stayed with them for two months straight. They got their fill of their toddler grandbabies in the Caymans.

Sam and I got a break because there would be no eyes on our babies from the media unless we allowed it.

Nan would try to find out if either of the babies had any special abilities similar to Sam. Once my youngest graduated from UVA, she went to Nan and Poppy's temporarily. They trained her in business and she got to bond with her baby siblings for awhile. They loved each other a lot also. This made Sam so happy. He knew Nan and Poppy would love his children the same as they loved him. Nan and Poppy took the babies to Jamaica and Cozumel to visit their other family members in the islands. We could not have prayed for better caregivers.

My youngest helped me distribute 3Seats and incorporated Tortuga as an American staple. She helped Tamia with a few of her shows, became famous around the world for her style of encouraging people to love themselves in spite of and to trust GOD. 3Seats did the rest. Our now six children were an awesome bunch.

I was in love with a special man that loves me and enjoyed my loving him. We thanked GOD every day.

Sam said without words,

'No matter what our plans are...

GOD plants us where He wants us to be...

When He wants us to be there

and chooses the road He wants us to take.'

I responded, '**The End is Not a Lie!**'

Our Deepest Fear

"Our deepest fear is not that we are inadequate. Our deepest fear is that we are powerful beyond measure.
It is our light, not our darkness that frightens us.
We ask ourselves, who am I to be brilliant, gorgeous, talented, and fabulous?
Actually, who are you not to be?
You are a child of God. Your playing small does not serve the world.
There is nothing enlightened about shrinking so that other people won't feel insecure around you.
We are all meant to shine, as children do. We were born to make manifest the glory of God that is within us.
It's not just some of us; It's in everyone.
And as we let our own light shine, we unconsciously give other people permission to do the same.
As we are liberated from our own fear, our presence automatically liberates others."

By Marianne Williamson

www.ingramcontent.com/pod-product-compliance
Lightning Source LLC
Chambersburg PA
CBHW051834170626
46807CB00003B/1170